ON A SUNBEAM

ALSO BY TILLIE WALDEN

Spinning

The End of Summer

I Love This Part

ON A SUNBEAM

TILLIE WALDEN

Published by First Second
First Second is an imprint of Roaring Brook Press, a division of
Holtzbrinck Publishing Holdings Limited Partnership
175 Fifth Avenue, New York, NY 10010
fiercereads.com

Library of Congress Control Number: 2017957414

Paperback ISBN: 978-1-250-17813-8
Hardback ISBN: 978-1-250-17814-5

First edition, 2018
Book design by Andrew Arnold and Molly Johanson

Printed in China

Paperback: 10 9 8 7 6 5 4 3 2 1
Hardcover: 10 9 8 7 6 5 4 3 2 1

Drawn on 9x12 Canson Bristol board with a ragtag collection of Faber Castell pens, Uni Pens, and some pens I got in Japan that I don't know the name of. The coloring and cleaning up was done in Photoshop CC with a very tiny bamboo tablet that, despite all odds, continues to survive.

CHAPTER 1

That ship better be there...
Head straight through there. And tell Alma she owes me one.

um... hello...
Are you Alma or... is she here? I... think I'm in the right place.
AKTIS
GO
Wait! I...
THERE YOU ARE!
ABOUT TIME. Jesus, I'm gonna Kill Mel.
JULES! Get this ship closed up and tell Char to take off.
whaaat

But I JUST sat down.
JULES
FINE
It's Mia, right?
Yes. Are... you Alma?
That's me. Char, watch her for a minute while I help Ell.
This the new kid?
Yep. Mia- sit there.
Hey, Char, we're all closed up.
Hold on.

ALL RIGHT!
Everyone up here!
Char— quit hiding.
This is Mia, our newest addition.
Nice to meet you all.
This blond angel is Elliot, our very own mechanical genius.
Jules. What's up.

Jules, show Mia to your room. It's late and she must be tired.

um, Charlotte didn't introduce herself.
She heard my name already. She can figure it out.

Play nice, you two.
whatever
hi
You should be in bed now too, Jules.
It's 8:30, Alma, Jesus...

Alma's a bit of a freak about us getting enough sleep. Try not to argue.
Oh, ok
Oh, and Ell doesn't talk. No one told me that when I got here and I felt like an idiot. And they're non-binary.

No one told you?
I mean, they didn't do it on purpose.

Alma, Ell, and Char have been together for ages. They didn't think about it.

That one's yours.
cool

I'm glad you're here. I've always felt like an outsider 'cause those three are so tight...

How long have you been here?
A year-ish. Never thought I'd be on a team that restores old buildings, but it's better than being in School.
How'd you end up here? Alma didn't tell us anything.

Dunno, really... It happened at the last minute...
It's chill, doesn't really matter. You're here now.

You should get to bed, Alma's gonna check. Ell and I will be in soon.

GET UP, MIA!
Hurry up! Or we'll miss breakfast!
hup, hup, hup

Ahh, it looks GREAT!
eat up
Pass the cream.
What's the deal with the new job?
Jules, don't take all the bacon!

Where you going?
We're close to landing and I'd rather not crash.
It's an old religious site that's gonna be a museum.
Is it fucked?
Very. Everything is falling apart. We have a lot of work to do.

I WANT TO SEE IT FIRST.
did we crash?
Just a rough landing.

FIRST ONE OUT WINS AT ALL THINGS EVER!

Not participating in the race?

nah

CHAR! OPEN THE DOORS!

Just take it one day at a time, kid. You'll adjust.

Maria told me you're a quick learner.

GAH! CHEATER! NO PUSHING!

Keep your eyes open and you'll be fine.

This'll be a fun one.

5 years earlier

Mia

We're going.

If you don't hurry you'll be late...

Not. Going.

Um, assembly isn't **optional**.
It's the first day... you can't start cutting class already...

I'm not cutting **class**, it's assembly. No one takes attendance at assembly.

They check the rooms. They'll catch you...

whatever

cnk

Let's move the mats for tryouts—
HEY!
YOU SHOULDN'T BE IN HERE!
HEY
shit
Where'd she go?
I'll check here.
fucking hell
Mia.
Oh, hey, Ms. Martinez.
Why aren't you at assembly?
Well, you know... I, uh...
THERE SHE IS!
crap

Have a seat over there, Mia. Ms. Adams won't be pleased to see you starting off your year like this.
It was just assembly...
What're you in for?
Creative oppression.
What...?
Um.. uniform violation, I guess.
Jesus! Those shoes! Aren't those for, like, five-year-olds?
If they're for five-year-olds why do they come in MY SIZE?
Uh, giant five-year-olds, I guess.

You're new, aren't you?
If by "new" you mean to this school, then yes.

I'm Mia.
Grace.

Mia? Seriously, day one?
Look, you two, I don't have time for this. Detention for two weeks and I **don't** want to see you here again.
Excuse me, I have a few—
THANKS, MS. ADAMS.
Come **ON**
That's it?
Jesus, don't LINGER. Adams'll just keep going. And you better change those before class...
I suppose.

Your room is up here...?
Freshmen aren't on this floor.

Who are you rooming with?
No one.

NO ONE?! You got a single?? I didn't know we HAD singles.

You don't have to follow me.
I'm not.

Can I... see it?
No.
Just for a minute?

NO
SLAM

FINE! WHATEVER! I didn't ACTUALLY want to see it!

Hey
Hello
You wanna come eat with us?

No, thanks.
Seriously, they don't care. You can come.
I'd prefer to eat alone.

Could you please leave now?
I was just trying to be NICE, you freak.

It's almost lights-out.
I'll be right back.

Girls! Get to your rooms!
Grace!
It's me. Um, Mia.
Knock
I, uh...I'm sorry about earlier. I mean, you know, I...
It's okay.
I know I'm weird.
Do you... want to come in?
Now? Oh, yeah. Totally. Cool.
ONLY for a minute. It's almost lights-out.
Cool. cool, cool.
It's really nothing special.

Is it ok if I sit?
ok. I guess.
wow

CHAPTER 2
Hurry up, Mia! Char's waiting.
Jules, get the new tile from the ship. Mia, come over here.

Apply the sealant while I attach this.

Slow down. Yep, just like that.
Perfect.

Go help Jules with the tile. And bring down the extra stone while you're at it.

what am I doing?

You surviving?
maybe

Let's take lunch. I'll text Alma.
But Char said...
Don't worry. I'll tell 'er.

Meet me by the creepy prison thing.

Mia!
GAH

I got us, like, thirty sandwiches. And some coffee to pep you up.

I think I'm dying.
Dude, you're doing GREAT.

Took me months before I could get through a whole day without turning into jelly.

I don't think Char likes me...
hah
what??
You don't know Char.
But she's always laughing with Alma, then I show up and she gets... tense.
She's shy as hell. New people terrify her.
Seriously? She's SHY?
Usually she hides behind Alma when we meet new people. Just give her some time, she'll get used to you.
Huh. Okay.
Alma told you Char's the captain, right?
Captain?
Like, she's the highest ranked out of all of us. She's supposed to run the show.
It's not ALMA?
Nope, at least not officially. But Char lets Alma do it 'cause she hates being in charge.
Alma was obviously born for this job.
God, yeah. Char may have the degrees, but Alma knows how to yell.
Where's Elliot? I haven't seen them in, like, weeks, except in our room.
I have no clue.
Ell does specialized stuff. I don't really get it. They're—
JULES!
God, what, Alma?
YOU CAN'T EAT IN HERE.

It's not like we spilled—
This place is NOT our PROPERTY!
jeez..

Watch it. Now get this cleaned up immediately.
oKAY

Mia, go find Char. Lunch is over. Jules, you're with me the rest of the day.
right. okay.

This is SO dumb.

Pass me the light.

Hey, Char? Alma and Jules... are they...?
Don't worry about it.
Alma seemed really upset.

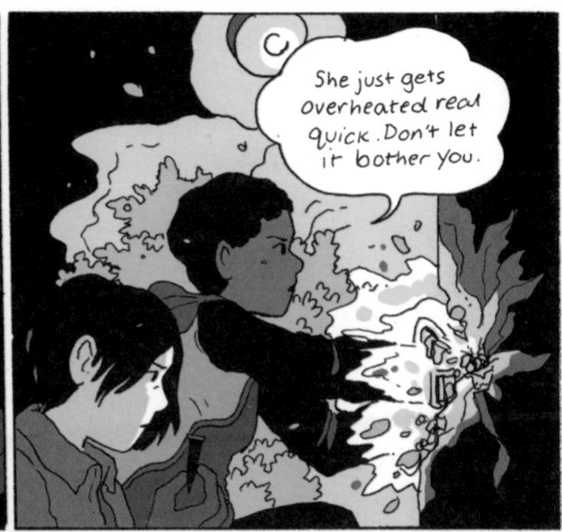
She just gets overheated real quick. Don't let it bother you.

You... wanna see inside here? I already finished it but I could still show you...
Inside WHERE?

Here.
It's a little small. This is the third hidden room I've found, though apparently there are hundreds.
...hundreds...?

Didn't Alma tell you about this place?
She mentioned it was some kind of church... like for some old religion.

It wasn't just old, it was **forgotten.** Almost all records of this place have been lost or destroyed.
I learned about a bunch of the new-wave space religions in school. I had a whole class on it.
Seriously? What kind of school did you go to?
Boarding School.
What School?
Uh... Cleary's School for Girls...
Wow, **ritzy**.
It's nothing. What's the deal with this place, anyway?
I don't know a lot. All I could figure out is basic facts. It was a small religion, only about 200 followers. They all lived here, supposedly. Each person had about ten rooms to themselves.
The central belief was all about finding this one object. They thought that holiness was tangible, and that the founder had hidden it somewhere in this complex.
That's why this whole place is full of tricks. Hidden rooms, stairs that lead nowhere.
They couldn't just... ask the founder where the thing was?
She died. And the rest of the group went crazy looking. Some thought the founder returned to The Staircase, where she was from, and never actually died.
Apparently a group went to The Staircase looking for her. And of **course** they were all never seen again...
What?
What...
...The Staircase. They really went there?

yeah...
and they... died
It's closed. No one can go in. But they risked it.
The imagery here does seem to support the idea that the founder had a connection there.
But it could still be rumor. Not many people actually manage to leave The Staircase.
No way...
It's strange to us, but for others... it's home.
I would've paid more attention to this place if I knew all this was going on...
I've been keeping track of all the information in my journal.
Oh, could I see it?
What? Oh... you don't have to... I mean, it's not part of your job to know that stuff.

I know. I just thought they'd be cool to see. If it's ok...
No, yeah, it's fine! I just... the others don't usually care about all this stuff.
We should probably get back to work...
'Kay
Wouldn't want the door to fall closed and lock us in here forever, right?
What?
I'm kidding! Joking. It was a joke...
Oh. Well I did actually have the same thought. I don't think the door is very stable...
YEP TIME TO GO

You CHEATER!
How did you get such a good hand?!

Don't give me that look. I can still win.

Hey.
Hey, dude. Come to watch me destroy Ell?

Is...everything good?
I'm golden.

You gonna sleep? We can play downstairs.
No, no. Just gonna lie down for a second.

HAH! Take this—LASER BEAM.

Mia
Time to get up. You're with me today.
Jules and Elliot?
Already working.

What time is it?

A little past five

How are you finding work?
Work?

It's... a lot more complicated than I thought. I knew I would be, you know, doing construction. But this feels like a lot more...

It is a lot more. We wear a lot of hats. Sometimes we're fixing walls, other times we're restoring art. Every job is a little different.

It can be frustrating, though. Every now and then we're hired to turn a place full of history into some shitty office space. That always breaks my heart.
But it also means we're often the last ones to see a place before it's gone. And Char keeps records of every-where we go. So even if it's gone, we won't forget.

I was sorta expecting to just do... hard labor... Like, mindless stuff.
Well, it is just labor when you get down to it. But if you want to find meaning, it's there.

Is there something else you want to ask me?
Are you and Jules okay?
Char told me you were worried.

Family is complicated
Wait, **family**?
You're kidding. She didn't tell you?

whoa
She'll probably Kill me for telling you, haha.
So Jules' mom is...
My middle sister. She died a few years ago, and I've been Jules' guardian since.
oh
I... don't always know how to take care of her.

Do we have all the pieces?
I'm making more popcorn.
How exactly do you play this?
We'll teach you as we go.

Wizard totally beats Cat.
Not ALL cats.
Yeah, scottish folds are powerful.

GAH! What a lucky roll!
You're not winning this time, Jules. My platoon is headed straight for the flying castle.
You're really competitive, Jules...

Former figure skater. It's in her blood.
Good lord.
SHHHUTUP
Ohhh

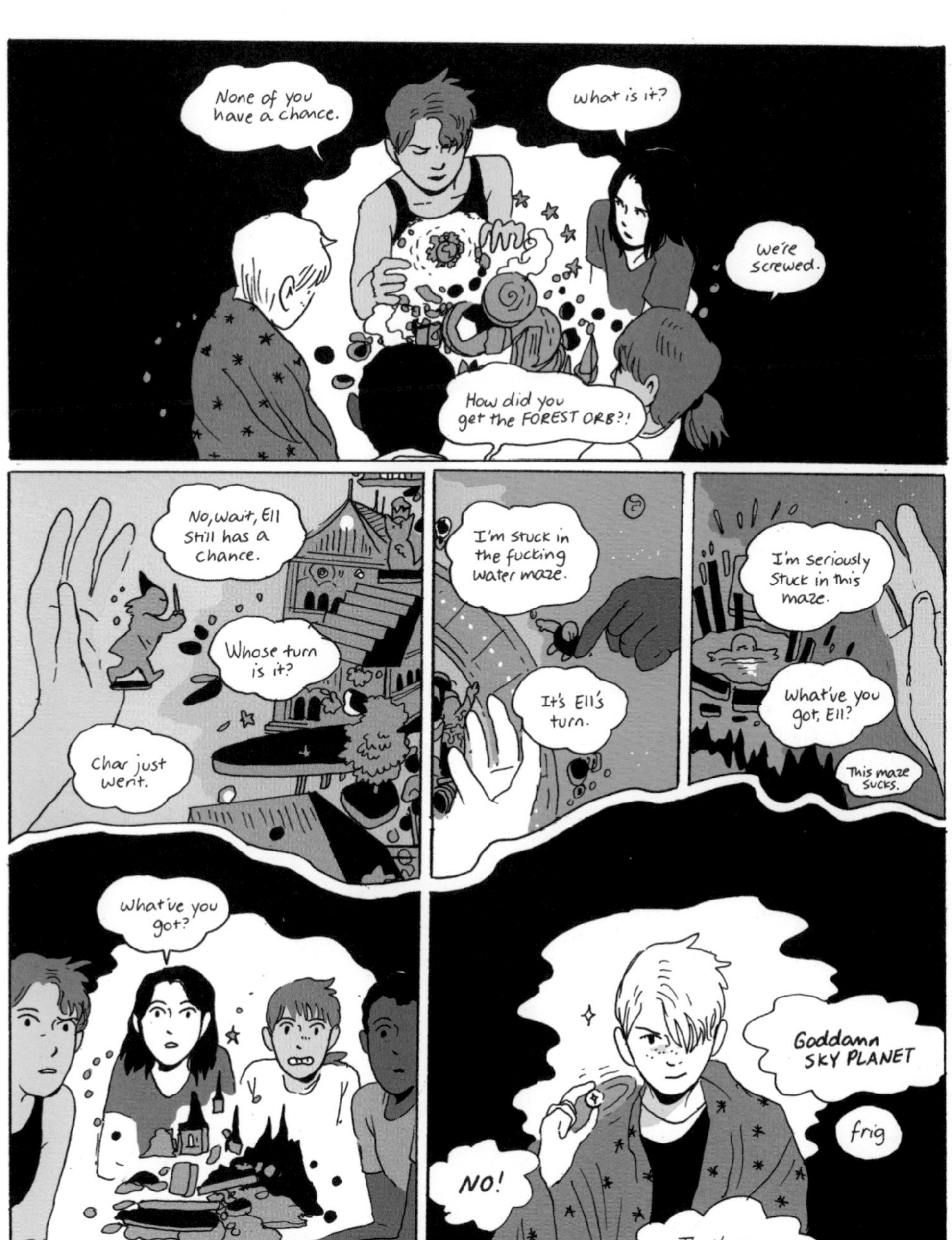
None of you have a chance.
What is it?
We're screwed.
How did you get the FOREST ORB?!
No, wait, Ell still has a chance.
Whose turn is it?
Char just went.
I'm stuck in the fucking water maze.
It's Ell's turn.
I'm seriously stuck in this maze.
What've you got, Ell?
This maze sucks.
What've you got?
Goddamn SKY PLANET
frig
NO!
That's an automatic win.

Well, what do you think?
I know it's late...
Just one more game?

CHAPTER 3

There was a large movement of young people to the rural fields area around Jupiter in the early '50s. Can anyone explain why?

Living was affordable and they were harvesting a resource in great demand!
Well PUT, Alex.

I want everyone to take out their edu-sets and watch the migration, taking notes on any patterns you notice!
ughhh
Dude, mine is broken.

Did you hear Crissy got kicked out?
No way.
Focus, please!

You ready?
Nnughhhow much longer do we have to do this?
Three more days.
guhhh
No sleeping in detention, Mia.
I'm just resting...
what are you doing?
writing
what are you writing?
Nothing
Doesn't look like nothing
IT IS
QUIET, girls.
come on, show me!
MIA. Final warning.
FINE. Fine. Excuse me while I REST.

That's all for today, girls.
Yessss
Mia, a word.
Noooo

You should really be using this time to catch up on your schoolwork. I've noticed a dip in your grades.
I'm trying.

Then try harder. I want to see you show some effort.
okay, okay

I've known you for more than three years, and you've always been a great student. Is anything going on?
No

Well, I'm here if you need me.

Were you listening?!
Yes.
ugh, GRACE. You do not have a future in espionage.

Come on, we've got like twenty minutes of free hour left!

Slow down, Mia!

I'm gonna show you all the cool spots that new kids don't know about. Think of me as your official tour guide.
I already took the official school tour.
I KNOW that, Grace. I'm gonna show you other stuff.
Please get down. That isn't safe.
Oh! You have to see the senior study room! It's so cool!
MIA!

Mia?
hmm?
Why are you hanging out with me?

I know you have other friends. I've seen you with them. Why aren't you with them now?
dunno
Do you really not know?
I mean, yeah, like I have friends but we're not **really** friends. They don't actually want me around. And I don't feel like faking it anymore.
And I mean, hanging with you has been...fun
Come on. There's another place I want to show you.

So that's the soccer team. They suck. Those side rooms are for yoga and stuff. And through the windows—do you see that tower?
Yeah, I see it.
That's where they play Lux.
Uh... Lux?
It's a Cleary original. You haven't heard of it?
Not at all.
Oh, MAN, you've been living under a rock...
It's our school sport. Basically it's a big treasure hunt for these colored orbs called planets. But you search for them in these crazy dark tunnels in ships that you get to build yourself! And every semester there's a HUGE tournament!
You sound like a big fan.
It's literally the coolest thing in this whole school.

You must play. Will you be in the tournament?
Me?? God, NO, no. Freshmen can't play. It's only for juniors and seniors!
Of COURSE not, that wouldn't...

Well, that's silly. You should play.
I can't!
Have you asked? There are always exceptions.
ASKED?

GRACE! Where are you going?!

GRACE
Pardon me, where is the Lux room? I need to speak to whoever is in charge.
The training tower? Through there. Ms. Miller is the coach.

Grace
Excuse me, are you Ms. Miller?
This is a closed practice, girls.
My friend here would like to participate in this sport. How can we make this happen?
You freshmen?
We may be freshmen but you can't put an age limit on passion and dedication.
No fish play Lux. We're full up, anyways.
She is willing—
HEY!
You're the kid who I caught sneaking in here. You've got some nerve.

Snuck in...right...
well, um

Well, YES, yes of COURSE she snuck in! She couldn't contain her passion! How could you turn away someone with such dedication!
No. Fish.

She'll do ANYTHING. Any task and she'll devote herself.

I guess I could use some help with cleaning and running supplies. It's not very glamorous.

Be here at five am tomorrow.
Five am
THANK YOU FOR THIS OPPORTUNITY

MIA WILL WORK HARD AND–
Come ON, let's go!

You're in!
I'm... in.
I can't believe it—you were amazing!
oh—I mean, I just...
oh shit
Miaaa!
What?
Grace, just don't say ANYTHING, just, just stay calm and—
Miaaa, it's been so long. How have we not talked yet this year?

Hi, I'm Grace. Who are you?
Wow, look at this one.

Grace, be quiet—
No, no, that's okay.

Wow, Mia. It is just so nice of you to be a guardian for the mentally ill. You're doing God's work.

Are you implying that I have some sort of disability?
Wow, good JOB. Did all that thinking give you a headache?

You're very rude.
GRACE

Get off of me!
You know that really hurts my feelings. I'll take your necklace. That'll make me feel better.

It isn't yours! You can't just take it!
haha
Get her blazer!

Grace
Grace, are you okay?
I need my necklace.
I know.
It has my powers in it. I need it back.
Okay. um, okay.

I'll get it back. I promise. I'll get your powers back.

CHAPTER 4

You comin' to bed?
mhmm
Are Char's journals really that interesting?
mhmm
You're not listening to me, are you?
What?
Don't stay up too late, you scholar.

* last place founder was seen

You SAID that to her??
She was an idiot! Like 'cause her dress was sparkly she thought it made her president of the galaxy.

Dude, even her SHOES had glitter.
Focus, you two.

Everyone's giddy because it's the last day, but that doesn't excuse slacking off.
We knowww.

Oh my god, I cannot believe Alma wants to keep this head...
Well, it's not going in our room. We have enough creepy statues.
What now?
Gotta find Char, help her pack up tools.
I still haven't seen Elliot, like, ANYWHERE.
Yeah, dude. They work on the circuits or something. Crawling between walls and floors and fixing stuff.
How do they fit?!
Dude, I have no clue.
Jesus, where is Char?? She's not responding.
We can try the next floor.
Hey—we didn't work down there.
Nope. We only have to fix what the museum wants. Another crew deals with the rest.

She's finally calling me, god.
Hey, where are you?
WHICH fountain? There's like fifty.
Yes, we put the giant head in the ship.
It's just like the drawing...
Could you **please** tell your girlfriend that we do not need all this junk on the ship?

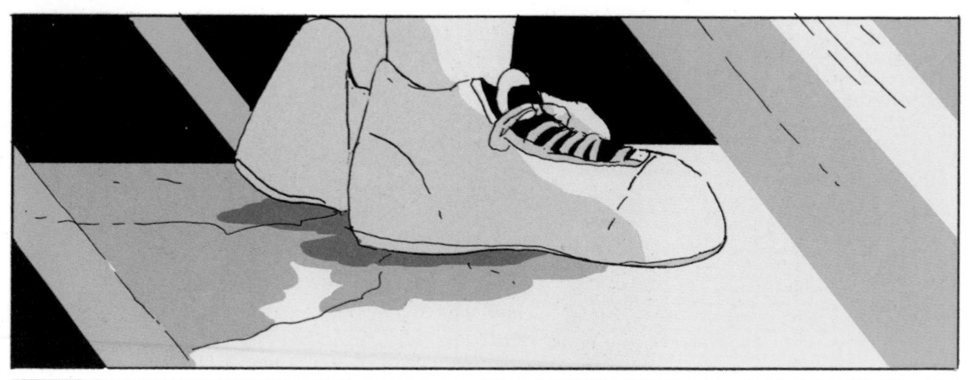

Aktis is already FULL, we... we...
Mia?

MIA!
Jules??

Jules?
Mia, get out of there!
It's not safe! We never stabilized this area!
Alma
hm?

Come on, you room together. You HAVE to know.
I can't go through her stuff, Mia. She'd kill me.
Please, just a quick look. A small gold neck-lace with a green stone.

I'll try. But no promises.
Thank you.

Mia, go collect the used planets in the ground tunnels.

Take it slow. The boards are not toys.
Have you seen Grace? I couldn't find her at lunch.
Maybe try the library?

Grace! I need to talk to you!

I have to get to drama club. Can't it wait till free hour?
This is important.
Fine. Talk fast.
Ok, so like, um, well, you have your writing and you're so good and I, like, want—
MIA.
Sneak into Lux tower with me at night so I can practice flying and catching planets.
That doesn't sound like a good idea.
No, it is! It is!
The only way for me to get good at Lux is if I practice. Then when I've gotten super good I can prove to Coach Miller that I should have a spot on the team!
hmm.
Say yes.
Why do you need me? Can't you do this dangerous escapade on your own?
I... I dunno. I just thought, whatever. It was dumb.
No, wait. Let's do it. I've read that life experience helps with the authenticity of your prose.
Uh, what?
Um, I never do anything crazy. So... maybe I should try it out.

I'll come by your room at two. I know how to get into the tower without getting spotted.
I'm terrified.
I'll be waiting.
You gotta jump!
Grace, come ON.
I could've broken my ankles!
You're fine, You're fine.

This is the one I've always wanted to fly.
Are you SURE you know how to do this?
I've watched the other girls start them up thousands of times. I can totally do it.
Ok, so take the bag of planets and put them in the chute. They'll go into the tunnels and I'll catch them
We shouldn't do this
Come on, we have to try!
Stay back.

BE CAREFUL!

Throw in the planets!
I'm going in!
Mia—

shit

Shit!
chk
shit
Don't move, Mia...
I'm coming.
CK
crk

Mia?

I can't—I can't
hold you...

MIA!
Jules!

Is your ankle...?
It's fine.

What... the **hell** were you two doing?
sit
ow

Alma.
Char.
Hold off for a minute.

Give them a second to breathe.
I don't GIVE a SHIT. They just DESTROYED—
It wasn't Jules' fault! It was all me! I—

Mia, we can talk about this later. We need to ice your ankle. Alma and I will get the first aid kit.
Oh, will we?
Alma, she's in pain.

You two stay **right** here. We'll be right back.

We're ok, Ell.
Just an...
accident.

I'm so
sorry, Jules.

Ah, man, it's
ok, it's ok.
C'mere

Mia...

Mia!
Grace!
Where are you?
Mia!
Grace!

What happened?!
I crashed!
oh god oh god oh NO, This is the end
Grace—
oh no oh no
Grace! We have to get out of here
But... which way? I don't know where we are...
Then we'll just start walking.

We'll make it out eventually.

CHAPTER 5
I could tell the teachers and you'd get expelled.
Go for it.

Today we'll be talking about Deep Space.

It's a region in the southwestern corner of our galaxy. Who can tell me the three main regions? Susie?

Willows, Bat Wings, and The Staircase.
Very good.

Now who can talk to me about why these districts are so dangerous?

No one?

Grace
Go AWAY.
You and your girlfriend have a fight?
haha
Grace, come ON. We need to talk.

They're gonna find the ship today. You have to have your story straight.
I'm going to tell the truth.
You can't!

Mia, could you come with me?
I don't know what you're talking about.
Mia, be serious. What happened last night?
Uh... I slept? Exciting stuff.
Coach Miller has told us She's Caught you Sneaking into the tower before. What do you have to say for yourself?
Wow, really?
The door was unlocked so I just walked in. And Coach Miller freaked.

Have a Seat, Grace.

Miaaa

Hey, shithead.
hahaa

Your girlfriend started bawling during study hall.
It was GROSS.

Guess you haven't figured out how to treat your women yet...

You cool?
Can you do me a favor?
Sure, man.
Tell my roommates I'm in the infirmary. They don't have to wait up.
yeah, ok.
Are you sick?
Mia?

Where's my shoe?
Do you have the answer to #6?
Shit, I never did that sheet.
Um, excuse me?
Mia?
This isn't your room, fuckface. If you want to live, I'd leave now.

Where is it?

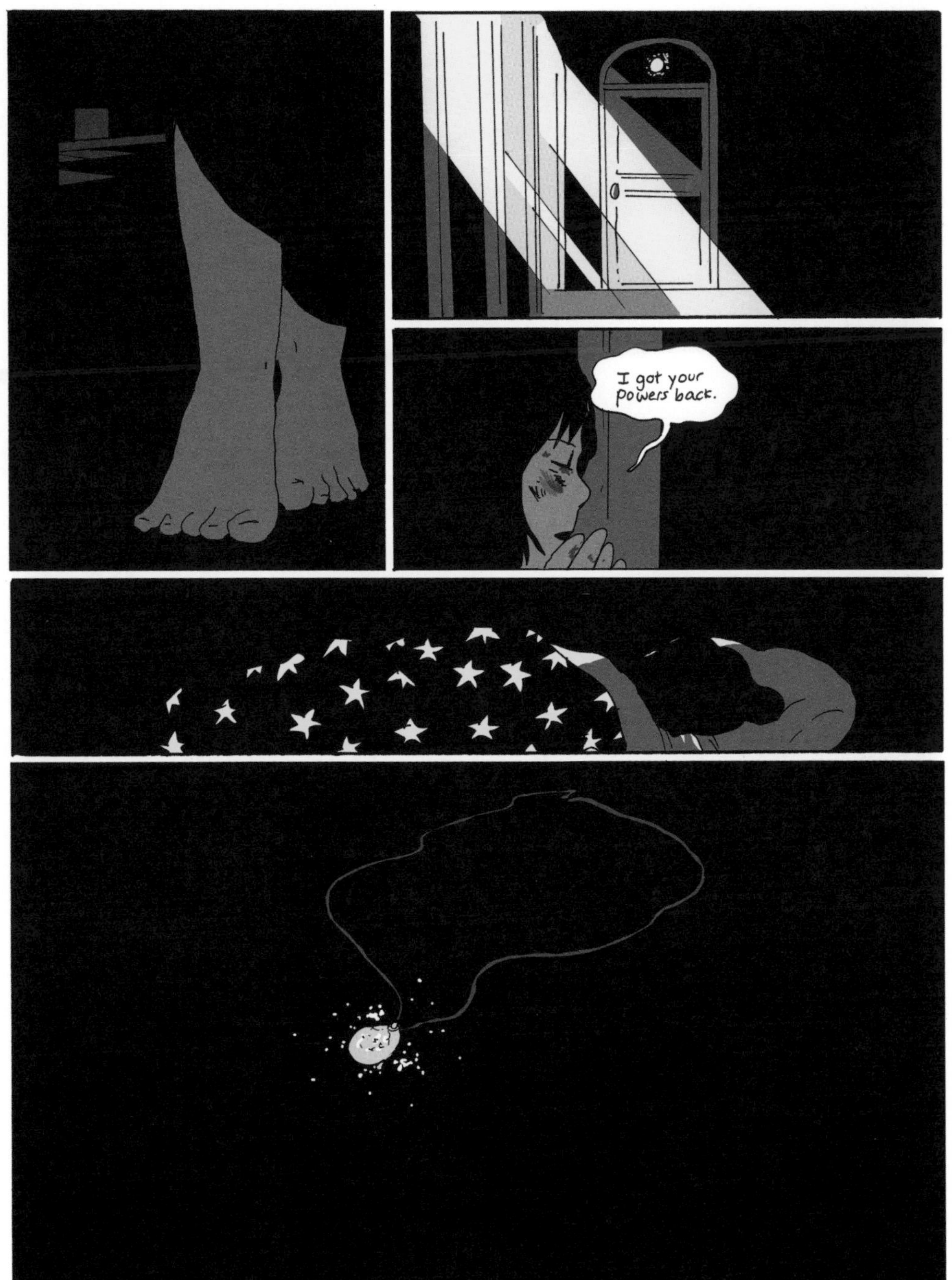
I got your powers back.

Do you understand what happens next? What this could mean?

no
What was that?
No. I don't know.

If we decide to report the incident, which we are required to do, it puts Char's whole career on the line.

Your mistake was under her watch, and for some fucked-up reason, she's the one who has to pay for it.
I didn't mean, I mean, I never thought—
Don't give me that bull-shit.
WHY did you go back there?! I know Jules explained to you that the areas I tape off are off-limits.
I dunno.
You DON'T KNOW?
I don't know, I was BORED or something. I DON'T KNOW.
Christ.
What's going to happen?
A few things.

The damage will be taken care of by another crew. We'll wrap up our work and leave tomorrow night. Char will file a report that you'll need to sign.
On our way to the next job, we'll stop at headquarters. I'll arrange for a ship to take you home.
no
Alma.
Not now, Char.
ALMA.
We aren't finished, Char.
I'm the CAPTAIN, Alma, in case you needed me to remind you.
Mia, give us a minute.

She's a liability, Char. What if something like this happens again?
Come ON, she's no more reckless than Jules. Don't exaggerate.

She destroye-
Why didn't you tell me where she went to school?
What?

All you told me when she came was that she went to boarding school. You didn't tell me which school.
Char, why are we talking about this?!
It's the school from that... job... isn't it?

I didn't want to bring it up. I know you didn't like that job...

That's an understatement. It was an insane risk.
But we didn't get caught.
It left Elliot shattered. You always forget that part.

Oh, GOD, Char, WHY are we digging this up?! We should be talking about Mia!
I don't know... I guess... well, we messed up a lot at her age, too. We should cut her some slack.
We hardly **messed** up. We knew what we were doing.
I know. That's the problem.
You're saying you don't ever miss that life?
You know I like what we have now... Steady paychecks, **legal** jobs... I don't miss the danger.
But I know you do.

Jules—close the ship up.

Come onnn. You have to eat, Mia. You'll just be more miserable if you're hungry.
Jules...
It's been two weeks. No more sulking is allowed.
OK, WHAT'S THE DEAL?
Jules-
Jules, inside voice.
Mia said that YOU said that she's leaving. And I said that my tía isn't a soulless monster. So, WHAT'S THE DEAL?
It's ok, Jules...
Alma, we should talk to them.

You want to explain, or should I?
mmm, you. Now there's too much pressure.

ALL RIGHT, everyone sit down and listen UP.

First things first, Mia. You won't be leaving us.

But your job will be changing. We'll have a chat about that later.

and...
What?

Char is going to file a report. With Mia staying, it's too risky not to.

No... Char...
you can't...

I'll be fine. You guys don't have to worry.

OKAY, enough of this. Jules, Mia, get plates. Ell, help me with the chili.
I set the table LAST NIGHT. Why me??
Let's use paper plates so we don't have to do dishes...
NO PAPER PLATES.
Let's go, you two!
God, I'm starving.
Alma, can I have a beer?

Mia
I'm awake.
Take a walk with me.
Did we land at the new job?
About an hour ago.
THIS is the new job?
Not all our jobs are glamorous. This old office is going to be turned into apartments.

I owe you an apology. I shouldn't have said...
It's OK, Alma. Really.
You forgive easily, don't you?
I've heard that before...
I appreciate it, Mia. And I must say I'm impressed.
I've never seen anyone charm Char the way you have. But she's totally rooting for you.
really??
OK. Here we are.

Starting today, you're Ell's assistant.
Read this all and learn it. It'll cover the basics.
I...don't even know what Ell does..
They work on the technology that makes the buildings fly. Ell's work keeps these walls together.
But I-
Head in here.
Ell's waiting.
Work hard for me, Mia.
Ell?
Elliot?

CHAPTER 6

CHAPTER 7

I can't get this.

I read that chapter you showed me. About how I should think of all the circuits and wires like they're roads.
And that it's all like one big map.
Every part is unique, but they're all connected.
I think I sorta get it...
You're improving!
Thanks, Ell.
You're a great teacher.

We gotta eat something, Ell. We've been at this for eight... maybe nine hours.
HEY!
You two missed dinner!

Jesus, Jules. It's, like, two am...
I KNOW. I waited up so I could yell at you.

Alma and Char are SO BORING. It's like torture without you guys.

Oh, come on, it can't be that bad.
You have no idea.

Alma was just like "Omg, babe, let's have a glass of wine and talk about our day" and Char's like "omg, babe, yes." And I had to listen to that for, like, an HOUR.
Yeah ok, that sucks.

It's not fair, Mia. I never see you anymore.
Aw, Jules. I miss you, too.

I blame you. You stole her.

Well, we can hang out now. Ell and I just need to eat something.
DEAL!

I WILL MAKE COFFEE
AND GET THE GAMES!

If we're gonna infiltrate, we need to do it NOW.
It's too risky.

Come ON, Mia. We can't just wait out here. Look, Ell is totally in.
All the entrances are blocked. It's Suicide.

We have to try! We've Survived this far.
OKAY! OK. Fine, let's do it.
I'll go in first. Then Mia, then Ell.

GO GO GO!
Shit! We're outnumbered!
CRAP! Jules, watch out!
I'M SO DEAD!
What do we do??
You and Ell have to keep going!
NO WAY! Ell, you have more healing than me— get Jules and meet me at the Diamond Bridge.
OK, good, I really didn't want to die.

Everyone ready?
We're going to slowly reattach the part of the building that fell off.
All good.
yeppers!
Let's do this.
First push!

Ready for the second one?
Wait, Jules!
We only have a few more.
OK! Go for it!
Slowly, Jules!

ALL RIGHT! Nailed it!
We still have two more wings to attach.
Could you NOT ruin my moment, Char?
Let's go, let's go. On to the next one.
What, we're going down there?
You bet.
Come on, Mia. We don't actually do this job to fix things. We do it 'cause we get to climb and jump off stuff.
That's pretty accurate.
Y'all are slow, I'm going now with or without you.

Aw, Char—
wait for me!
dammit
You got this. Just,
like, fall. It's easy.

Claire... you're being crazy. You should listen to Mom—

Shit
BZZZ
Ahh
CHAR, TURN YOUR PHONE OFF ohmygod
Mom... you're dating the HAIRDRESSER?!

YES, this is Charlotte. This better be good!
How could you, Mom?
Yes. I understand.
Char?

Ok. Thanks.
Hun?
I just got suspended.
WHAT?
What are—
Shh!
I KNEW IT! I knew it. We should NEVER have reported the accident. They wouldn't have found out!
We're not doing that anymore! You promised me we'd go by the book.
We're not those people anymore.
You say that like we used to be villains—
You know we crossed lines. Don't rewrite history.
I'll be back in a few months.

We're close, Mia.
CHAPTER 8

We just need to review for the history final.

I can't study anymore, Grace. I'm out of juice.
Just five more minutes.

Okay. Okay.
All right! Let's begin with the development of inter-planetary currency.
In what year did the gold nick go into production?

I can't do this.
Ok, that was a tough one. How about the first planet to use artificial stars?

It starts with an "e."

Then... an "a"...
Earth?
Yes! yes. Correct!

Grace, I'm screwed...
Let's... just get some rest. Tomorrow's a big day.

Thanks for helping me study.

You still like me, right? Even though I'm not smart like you?
You ARE smart, Mia. You just don't try hard.
But yes.. yes, I still like you.

OMG
oooooh
AWWW

Mia
Oh, hey, Coach Miller.
Can we speak for a moment?
uh, sure
You haven't been coming to Lux practice.
Oh, I mean... I'm not really on the team so I thought...
Don't worry about the crash, Mia. I know you weren't involved, that's all been taken care of.
That's not... I- I don't know what you're talking about.
It's really none of your concern. Just don't let all that business stop you from coming.
We have a practice Friday morning. We could really use your help cleaning the tunnels and getting ready for the tournament.

NAME: Mia Sagang
Short answer: Describe the establishment of the tea planets:

I totally screwed up the essay question.
How'd you do, Mia?
How do you think?
Come ON, guys, it's time for dinner.
Ohmygod, just forget about it. Think about tonight!
What did you put on that orange question?
D, all of the above.
Shit! I put A!
I'm gonna wear my bow tie!
Hey
Hey

Let's not talk about finals, ok?
Thank you.

Aaaah!
Hurry up!
Everyone is giddy.
Probably 'cause of the dance.
Dance?

Oh, right. I always forget you're still kind of new.
Dance?
Whenever there's a big test, the seniors throw a dance in the gym. It's tradition.

I just... I guess I just assumed you didn't want to go 'cause you didn't say anything...
Well you didn't say anything, either!
I mean it's just a dance, it's not a big deal...

Well... when does it start?
Eight... at the gym.

Pick me up from my room at 7:50. Don't be late.
Shit! Kris—I need your help!
Mia—what's up?
Are all the flowers gone? I know you did the orders!
They're all gone. You would've had to order them a week ago.
dammit
You didn't order one for Grace?
No, I-I didn't think we were going. Do you have any leads?
Try Abigail. She ordered a shit ton for her girlfriend. She might be willing to share.
You rock.
I owe you one.
You're good, dude. We're even after you helped me fake that note.

Abigail!
Hey! Watch it—
What's up, Mia?
You should be careful running in the halls, Mia.
uhh... What's up?
Hey, What the FUCK!
I'll pay you back!
Shit! I still have to get dressed.

I stole a flower from a girl and got dressed really fast so I don't look good and you look so nice and I still can't believe you're my girlfriend and I shoulda ordered you flowers and made you a card and—

Mia—
And I stole a hoverboard from the gym, cause I've always wanted to pick you up in my very own ship but I don't HAVE a ship, I only have a stolen hoverboard—
MIA!

Let's go to the dance.

Get OFF of that! What are you two doing?? No hoverboards outside the gym!

Grace?
hmm?
I think I need to turn myself in.
uh—what?
The... the Lux crash... Coach Miller told me Someone else is being blamed.
Mia—wait—
I'll get in so much trouble but I-I have to... I have to—
Mia, wait—

You don't have to do that—it's... it's really not a problem...
Not a PROBLEM? It was ME. It was all my FAULT, and no one else should—
Mia, it was ME. I took the blame. But you don't have to worry, I'm not in any trouble. 
What?
You—
How?

I mean...you never wondered? The crash? The fight? I got you out of ALL of that.

But **HOW**? How?!

I can't tell you..
I...
And...I wish I could, but I can't.
And I'm sure you think I'm making this up and you probably hate me now.

You're an IDIOT.
Excuse me?
I said you're an IDIOT.
You don't get it, do you?
um, I—
I like ALL of you, Grace. Even the parts I don't get yet.
I'm not dating the 12% of you that I understand, I'm dating 100% of you. Including all your secrets that I don't know.
So don't EVER say I'd hate you because that's stupid and not true.

Oh, Mia.
I'll tell you everything someday...

Grace!
Grace, come on! The dance is ending.
right

CHAPTER 9

This fucking sucks.

LADIES. There you are.
Shit

This isn't break time. You had a break two hours ago.
Are you stalking us, Jo?

All of you need to get back to work.
oh REALLY
come ON, Jules.

And MIA. Your hair is a hazard. It needs to be up. And Jules—
WHAT?

Tell me what's wrong with me. I dare you.
Is there a problem?
oh GOD
A PROBLEM? I have a list. NUMBER ONE: these stupid-ass uniforms.
I can't do this, Ell.

Char's only been gone a month. We'll all go crazy or get fired by the time she's back.

And all of it... it's my fault.

Sometimes I just wish... everything would slow down...

I fuck things up, or everything turns sour, and it just rushes by me.
And I'll take a second to catch my breath...
But by then it's too late. Everything.... everything is gone...

It's probably time to get back to work.

So, let's review for the day.

I would like everyone to tell me where they're at in their work. Then we will discuss the plan for tomorrow.

Elliot, would you like to begin?

I'm not sure what this is. Why won't she speak to me? Her file didn't mention any—
THEY. Not "she."

Elliot isn't the chatty type.

You are all on very thin ice. Your insubordination will be reported and there will be consequences.
NOW. Jules. Tell me about your work today.

Hmm. you know, it's really tough to remember, Jo.
But I'm sure you get that. You can't remember one person's pronouns.

Was that helpful, Jo?

Alma—what are you gonna do??
Why are you asking me?
We need to get Char back! We need a plan.
I'm going to bed.
Alma!
Elliot—
We need you.
There's nothing I can do, Jules.
Bullshit.

what do we do now?

Drink?
Absolutely.

Ugh, this tastes terrible. I love it.
I didn't know Alma would get like this without char...

Man, I didn't, either... But I guess they've never really been apart for long, so they don't know how to deal.

Plus she's not used to being so powerless.

How long have they... you know...
Dated? Ages. They met when they were teenagers, back when Alma was doing all that illegal flying shit.
Illegal flying?

Haha, Alma hates that I know about it. She's embarrassed now. So, remember those years when everyone was super into moving to all the unexplored areas of space? Everyone wanted to be a god-damn trailblazer...

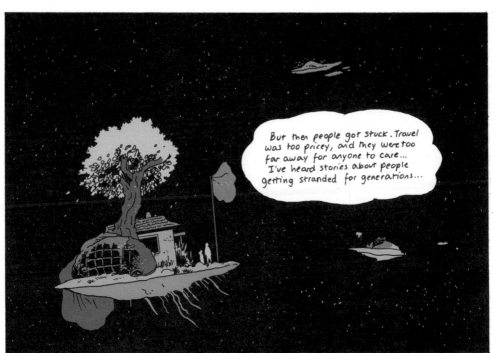

But then people got stuck. Travel was too pricey, and they were too far away for anyone to care... I've heard stories about people getting stranded for generations...

And Alma, she worked with this group that helped people get out. They flew everywhere, breaking every border law around.
She's been to some scary places. But wherever someone placed a flag for help, they went.

She met Char in the middle of it all...

Oh. Is that how they met Elliot? They all worked for the same group?
Elliot... No... not exactly.

Elliot... Elliot was one of their jobs. A flag went up somewhere in Deep Space...

There was Elliot. Waiting for them.

Yep.
I don't really know what happened next. All I know is that Ell stayed with them after that.

I used to ask Alma all the time about those years. About what they did together... but she wouldn't tell me.
Deep Space... You don't know where, exactly?
Nope. Ell doesn't talk about their past.

It still makes me angry sometimes.
Why?
It's just like... Sometimes it doesn't feel fair. I'll never have what they have...
No matter how much I try... I can't get in. It's...
Exclusive.

YES. Exactly.
I feel that sometimes.

But, you know. It's whatever. Alma took me in, even though she didn't have to.
Oh, right. I keep forgetting that...
She told you about my mom, didn't she?
She did, yeah. She told me—
HEY!
wait
Alma **LIED** to me. She told me...shit, what was it...that she was a doctor or something before this.
Oh, that is perfect.
I think she was in medical school for, like, a week.
Ahh, I totally believed her.
oh my goddd Mia
what what what
we have to **WORK** tomorrow
Shhhh

Why are adults so stupid?
hmn?
It's like the older you get the more you forget that you can **change** things.
Which is stupid because adults have money. Which means you can afford to buy a sledgehammer and break down the room you're stuck in.
Kids don't have sledge-hammer money...
Jules... where are we going?
Gotta check on Alma. She keeps going to sleep at her desk or the floor or something.
Gotta get her into her bed...

We're not supposed to go in her room.
We're not supposed to drink, either.
Jules—wait.
Shh
Come on, Paul. Alma needs some company.

Ell
Time to get up.

GOOD MORNING, ladies. Good to see you two taking initiative.
Hey—um, Ell.
I don't really know how to... how to say this.

Jules told me where you're from. About how Alma and Char...
I just... I—

I need a favor.

CHAPTER 10

All right, team! It's the big day! The tournament is in five hours!
We're gonna need an extra scale here.
The wing is too weak!
agh
yes! It works!
Where is the damn drill?
Kelsey, come ON.

Mia— who is this?
I got this.

This is Abigail. She's here to help.
You didn't run this by me.

Come on, Coach! Every ship needs to be polished for the game tonight. It'll take forever on my own!

Just for today.
You got it!

OK. We're even now.
hmm
Come ON. It was ONE flower.

True. Okay, we're even.
Hey! Mia and... Mia's friend—we need your help.

Polish the eyes and wings. Use this stuff.

Did you get your results?
oh yeah.

Totally bombed. Failed every section of the test except for biology... Gotta do summer school now.
Oh SHIT! Do your moms know?
Not yet.

Grace killed it, though. Second highest score in the whole grade.
She's AMAZING.
I know.

Hey, Mia— little help.
Sure thing.

ok, we're good.
thanks

Mickey, let's do the test ride.
we can't yet. The others aren't here...

Just take those two. We only need to test the weight.
hmmm.

Don't do anything. We're just gonna make a quick lap.
the Joulwan

...
......

Mia! You're late!
Sorry! Lux ran over!

You gotta change.

Faster!
Ahh

We'll go in for thirty minutes. No chatting, This is supposed to be exercise.

Remember, you can just click your watch if you need to come down and take a break.
You'll go in in pairs. Everyone get a buddy and form a line.
Ellen!
ow!
I got here first!
Be my buddy!
Connie!
Buddy!
Robyn!
Sari! buddy!
Gina!
Ok, in you go. Take it slow.
You two are getting marked tardy.
ahghhh
Go on in. Next—
uhh... I've never done this before.
Don't worry. It's easy.
Don't let go of my hand.
I won't.

You're fine! Just relax!
Don't let go!
I'm not! I've got you!

I've got you

Are you listening?
yes

But—but this is just the intro, ok? It just describes the world. You don't meet the characters until later...
I-I've never read this part to anyone before...
You don't have to—
No, I want to.
ok.
It looks like this.

A huge rock. A rock so big that it's a world. But it sits in a toxic place; a place where nothing is supposed to live. There are constant storms, star showers, and endless wind.
This climate wears the rock down. And someday it will be worn down to nothing.
They live at the top; the highest point. Not many people have homes on the surface. Most people live inside; kept warm by the walls and tucked away from the wind.
No one ever leaves. No one is supposed to, and no one really wants to. But there are people who watch just to make sure no one slips out.
But why would they want to go? Everything is here.
We have all six seasons, plenty of land and oceans of hot water. We have five cities and sixteen towns. We have tunnels full of every tree and plant and flower, and enough dust to smother the universe.

I love it... I'm kind of scared but I love it...
Really? You mean it?
Haha—no, stop! That tickles!
Oh—I'm sorry.
Oh, no, no. Not that kind of stop.
But you'll tell me, right? If you want to stop or slow down? You won't hurt my feelings.
I will.
You'll tell me, too, right?
You can do anything to me.

MIA, be serious.
I will. I'll tell you.
30TH ANNUAL LUX COMPETITION
PLAYERS:
They're coming!
Hurry up!
GO CLEARYS!
AHHHHH
Abigail!
Y'all made it!

ANDERSON SCHOOL

And here they are! Anderson School has arrived for the thirtieth annual Lux Competition!

The Cleary Lux Team is ready to go, led by our star player: 12th grader Soo Kim!
Grace—a moment of your time, if you could.
The Anderson team is led by 11th grader Aisha Lee.

The clock has started and the players now have two minutes to prepare their ships!
Soo Kim will be flying the three-wing, two-cylinder ship Neptune.
WE CLEANED THAT SHIP!

Thirty more seconds!

Grace! I cleaned—
Grace?

This just came for you.
Time is up! The planets are now being released!
The game will start in 3...
NEPTUNE
2...

1! And the game begins!
Grace?

One year earlier

I can't believe you're letting her leave.

Give it a rest, Jane.
Why? This is serious.

Mom, we're breaking our own laws. Our family decided a long time ago that no one leaves, and no one comes in.
!

Helen, go help Grace pack, please.
Fine.

You too, Mattie.
Fine.

I know the history, Jane. And I'm not changing our laws. I'm making an exception, and no one else needs to know.
But if people find out... it'll start a war.
And how do we even know she'll get out undetected?! She's—
The people I hired are no joke. They'll get Grace out safely.
But, Mom... She'll never come back.
It's just a few years of school. She'll come home.
No. I would come home. Mattie would, too, even Helen. But Grace?
no way.
Grace! What is this?
What?
You can't take all of those!
Well I can't leave them, either.

Grace...

You really want to do this?

yeah.

Mom's not happy.

she said YES.

You didn't give her much of a choice with your hunger strike...

You are not seriously bringing all those books..

Leave us alone, Mattie.

She can stay.

Oh—Grace, you cannot bring this.
No. No way.
what? Why? I like that.

Way too Staircase. You gotta dress like an Earth kid.
You gotta look cool.
Cool? Oh!

My light-up shoes! These are the coolest thing I own.

Right. Perfect.
Super cool.

God, you still have this Sweater? Didn't this used to be Jane's?
We've all worn that old thing... Don't bring that.
No, I like it! It... Smells like home.

Oh—you need a nice dress! Take Mattie's blue one, that should fit you soon.
You can't take that hat. But here, take these shorts.
I don't need Mattie's stupid dress...
Take it. Just in case.

OK. Where's your knife?
You can take mine.
Ugh, Helen! It's SCHOOL. I don't need a knife.

Well, then, what will you use for protection?
Take mine, Grace.
Ahh No! What!

Oh! I gotta bring America.
AMERICA?
My bear.

Grace... you'll get picked on if you bring that.

See? That's exactly why you need the knife.
Solid point.

Knives probably aren't even ALLOWED.

Well, then hide it in America.
Here, I'll rip a hole.
AHHHH

Grace—I'm kidding.
You were?

I'm putting a knife in your trunk.
Take America.

Grace! It's time!
Hold on—I'm finishing her hair.
mew
shh
Dammit, Grace, this is ALL books isn't it?!
How exactly does this work?
They'll come wherever the flag is.
What if they don't show?
They will.

Grace, c'mere.
I got something for you.
What is it?
A necklace. I want you to keep it with you. Always.
Why?
It's...magic.
Will it give me powers?!
Sure. yes.
Keep it close, ok?
I will.
You're mean. She actually believes you.
At least now she'll hold on to it.
And we can keep track of where she is.

Grace!
They're coming!

You must be Grace. Ready to go?

Take this route exactly and you should get out with no problems.

And don't delay. Within a few hours the mountains will move and the path will be blocked.

Time to go, Gracie.

You're good, Ell. They didn't see you.
But just in case the kid recognizes you, you'll have to stay... hidden, for a bit.
I'm sorry. I know it's hard to see this place again.
We won't ever come back, OK?
They'll never catch you.

Jane, where are you going?
Jane!
She's fine!

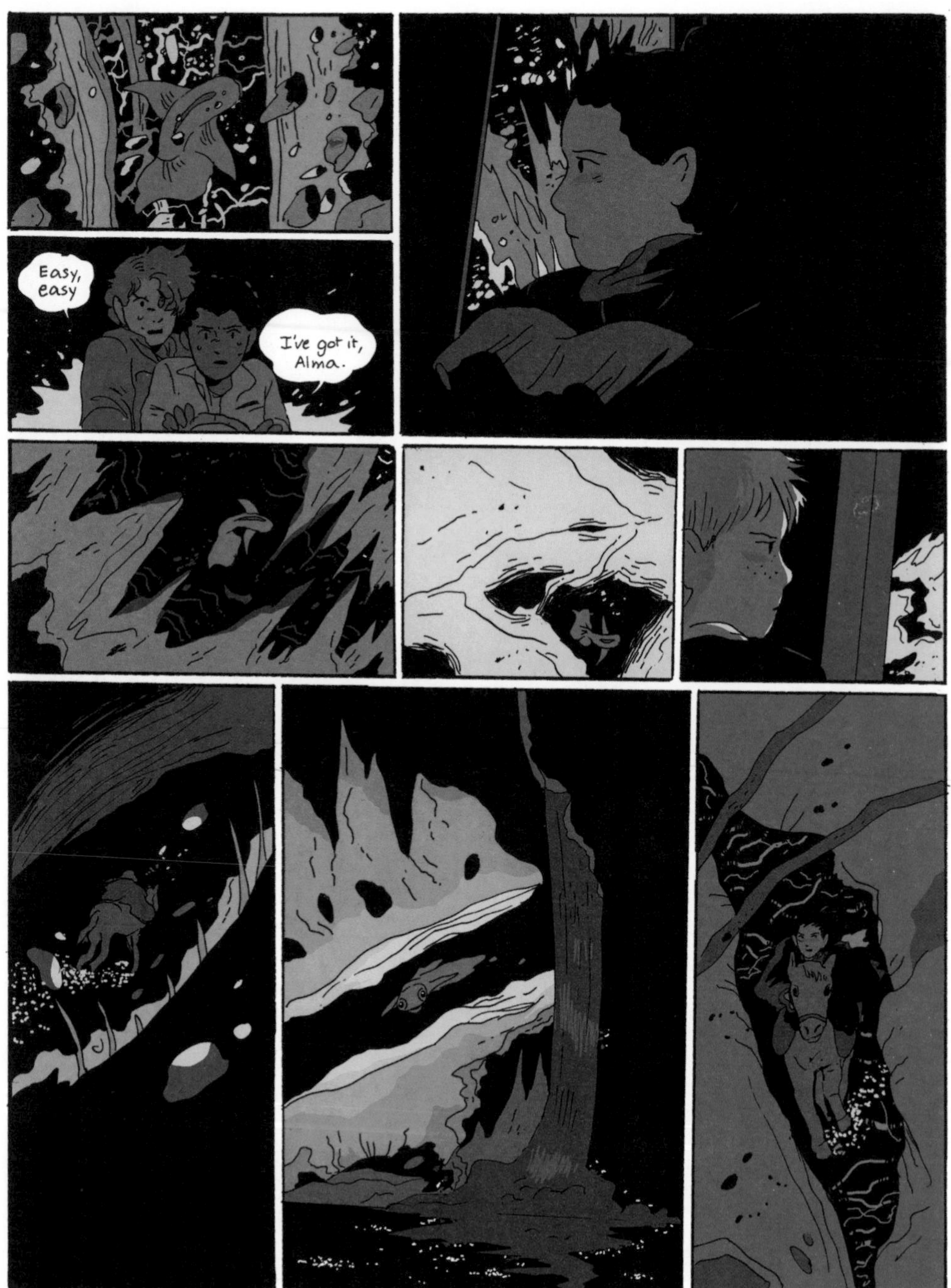
Easy, easy
I've got it, Alma.

There's the border! We're good!
Bye, Grace.

We're here.
I'll get her bags.

Thanks.
You can keep my cat, Paul. I don't think he's really allowed here.
That's the most she's said to us this whole month.
What're they thinking? The Hills sending their youngest to school **outside** The Staircase?
I'm just glad we got her here. If anything had gone wrong... well, Ell wouldn't be the only fugitive anymore.
Welcome to Cleary's, Grace.

What're you in for?

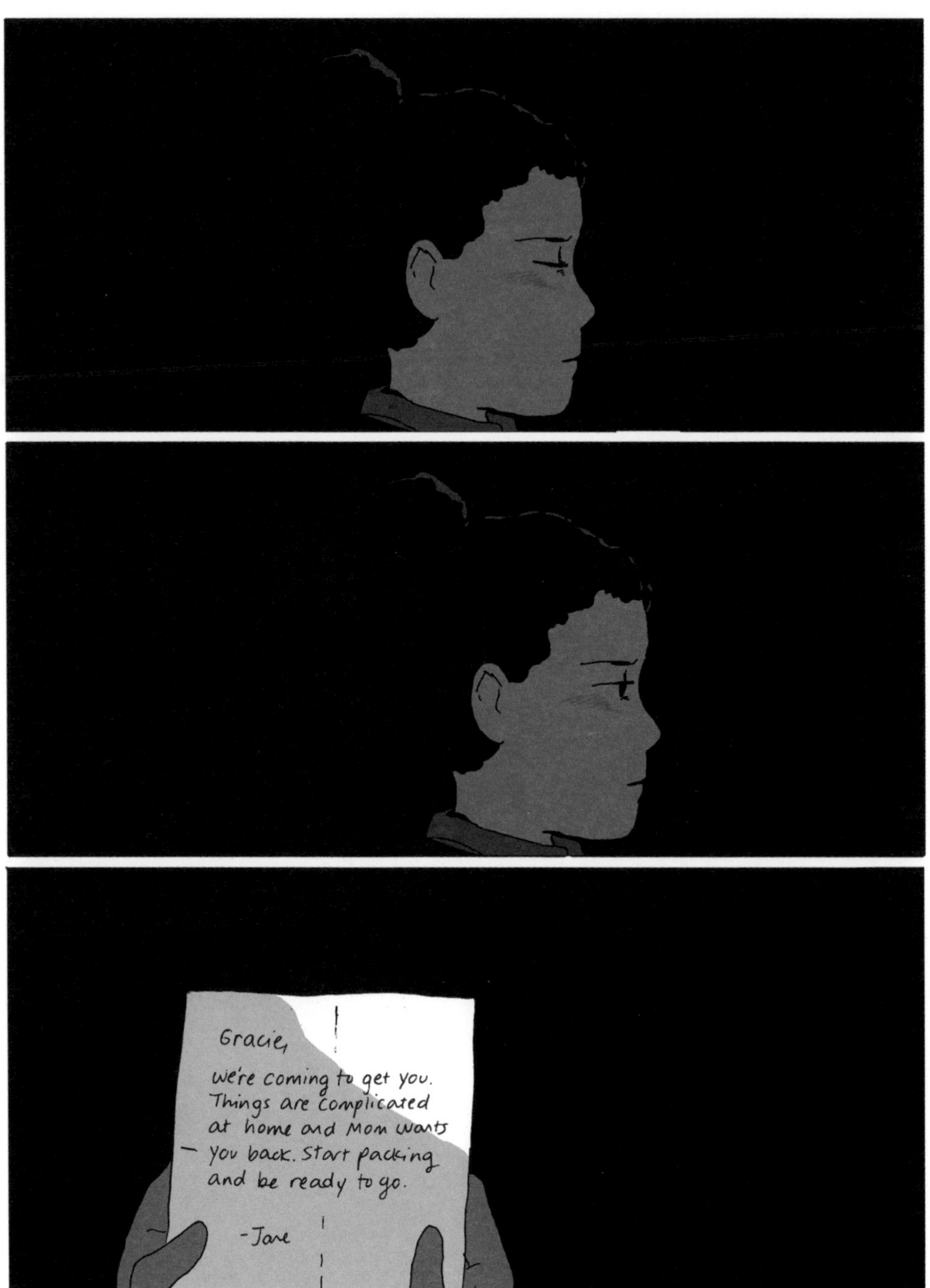
Gracie,
we're coming to get you. Things are complicated at home and Mom wants you back. Start packing and be ready to go.
-Jane

What've you got?

They only know where one of the sisters is?
I guess it's better than nothing.

I gotta think about what to do next.
CHAPTER 11

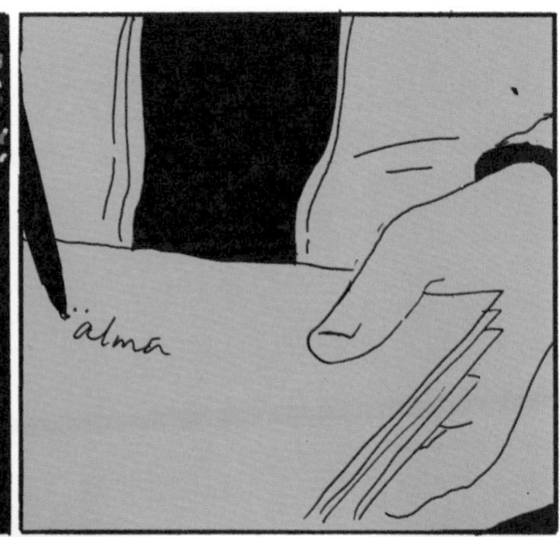
älma

Ah, shit. I don't know, Ell...

You really think that's the best move?

Fuck, if you say so. Let's go find her.

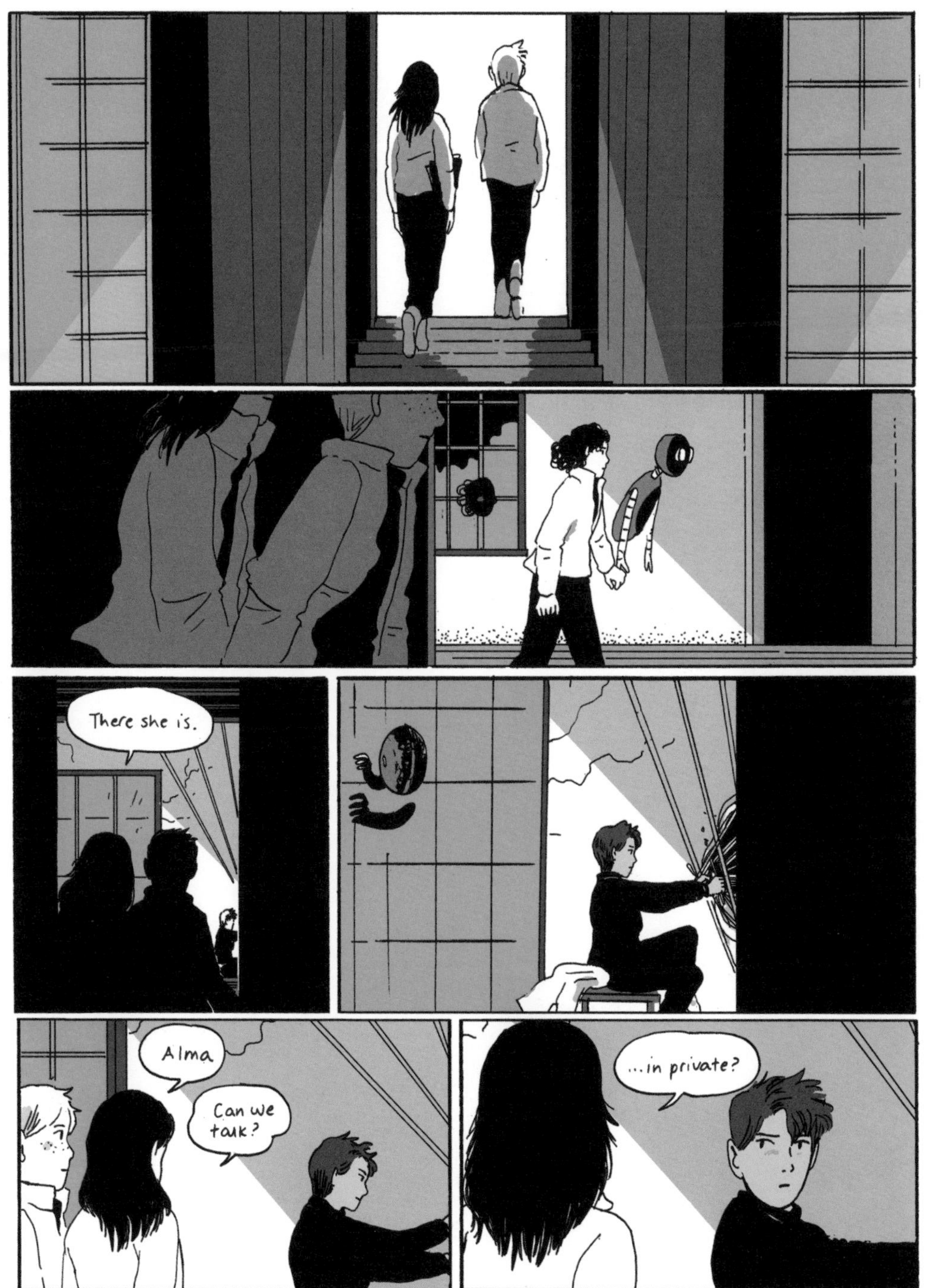
There she is.
Alma
Can we talk?
...in private?

We should be fine in here.
I guess... well, I need your help.
I'll... need a little more info than that.
tell her the whole story
Ah, jeez. OK. OK.
Well, it—
FUCK
SLAM
What the HELL?
AAAH

Keep your voice DOWN!
A SECRET MEETING?!
Jules..

How did you—
I'VE been following you and Ell. You two are UP to something.

Mia has something to tell us, Jules. And please, GOD, let's keep it down so Jo doesn't hear us.

Mia? Whazzup?
ahh

Fuck. You know what, whatever. I'll tell you. Just listen.

I... was in 9th grade. Boarding school. It was toward the end of the year when...

Gracie,
We're coming to get you. Things are complicated at home and Mom wants you back. Start packing and be ready to go.
-Jane
It's a message from my family. It just came.
Why didn't they just... call you?
It's complicated.
What does this mean?
I think... my sisters are coming to get me.
Sisters?
I have three. They're all older.
Mattie, Helen—
Jane.

Is this because you got in trouble for me?!
No.
Then... can you tell me now?
Tell you what?
Everything.
ok.
Im... I'm from The staircase.
hah!
what?
no
It's more than that, really.
The staircase... it's ours. My family sort of runs it. Or owns it, I guess.
H-how...
We have since the beginning. We founded it.
And I was the first to ever leave.
The principal knows. That's why I can't ever get in real trouble. She's... scared of me. Of my family.

Oh, GOD, Mia—
Say something
The... the staircase..
I.. didn't know that place was even..
What?
...real. I thought... it was all just a story...
Oh my GOD, it's REAL, Mia
It's real.
What're we gonna do?

That's easy. We'll just tell them you won't go.
I... don't think that'll work.
Well they can't MAKE you go.
I mean, summer break is in a month anyway. Just tell them you can come home for summer.
And then you can come back when school starts up again.
Right?

Right.

I... need some air... you're missing the game, too.
We can figure this out later.

ANDERSON
1,892
CLEARYS
1,964
DAMN, where have you BEEN?! The game's just ending!
Dude, HELLO?
We won!

We WON!

Mia! Shit—
Kris, help me out! Mia is sick.

Jesus...
You can't tell anyone, Abby.
I won't.
But... Grace said you were right, right? That she could just go home for summer.
She was lying.
Are you guys alive in there?
Like, maybe?
I'm fine, I'm fine.
Hurry up! It's the closing ceremony!
You guys go ahead.

You sure, Mia?
I'll see you around.

What's her deal?
Grace is leaving school.
No WAY.
Don't tell anyone.
Why is she going?
Dunno. Mia wouldn't say. But everyone knows Grace has something going on...
Hey, did you hear?
Hmm?
Mia, the kid who cleans the ships. Her GF got expelled.
No shit.
What's up?
Cleaner's GF got sacked.
Maya?
Mia
No shit.
Hey! Cristine!
WHAT do you want?
Come on, give your big sister some credit. That girl you had a spat with— turns out her girl got the boot.
Grace?
Think so.
You better be serious.
Duh. Thought you'd like to hear that.

It's about fucking time.
Looks like christmas came early...
I mean... is she even worth it at this point?
Are you joking? That bitch thinks she can get away with storming US? The only reason she's alive is because her girlfriend has the principal in her rich little pocket.
Not anymore, though.
I know exactly what to do.

Mia, you gotta get up.

Good morning! We have an important announcement, girls.

Due to the storm coming tonight all evening clubs and study halls are canceled.
Remember, girls! Report directly to your dorms after dinner!
Class dismissed.

Mia!
Not NOW!

Mia, please! I need to talk—
Fuck OFF!

You're here.
This is where I always meet you.
I know. I just... I thought...

It was just a long day.
We have an hour till dinner. What should we do?
Let's just go to your room.
The storm is starting.

But, like, isn't it a really long trip?
I guess. Depends on the ship and traffic and...
Well, then, that's great!
Your sisters won't get here for ages, then.
Plenty of time to make a plan.
I guess.
CRACK
FUCK
This storm is NUTS! How does this not freak you out?!
We had storms back home all the time.

Sometimes they'd last for months. They don't scare me anymore.
CRASH
WHERE ARE YOU GOING?!
Uh, to pee.
DON'T LEAVE ME!
CRICK
AAHHH

Here.

Turn around.

This'll keep you safe.
How?

Magic.

Magic. Got it.

CRACK

See? I told you it had a latch.
We're not here to break any goddamn windows.
Shh!
Could you move? I'd like to get out of this storm.
You think she's here?
Close the window!
SHHH

Who the fuck is that?

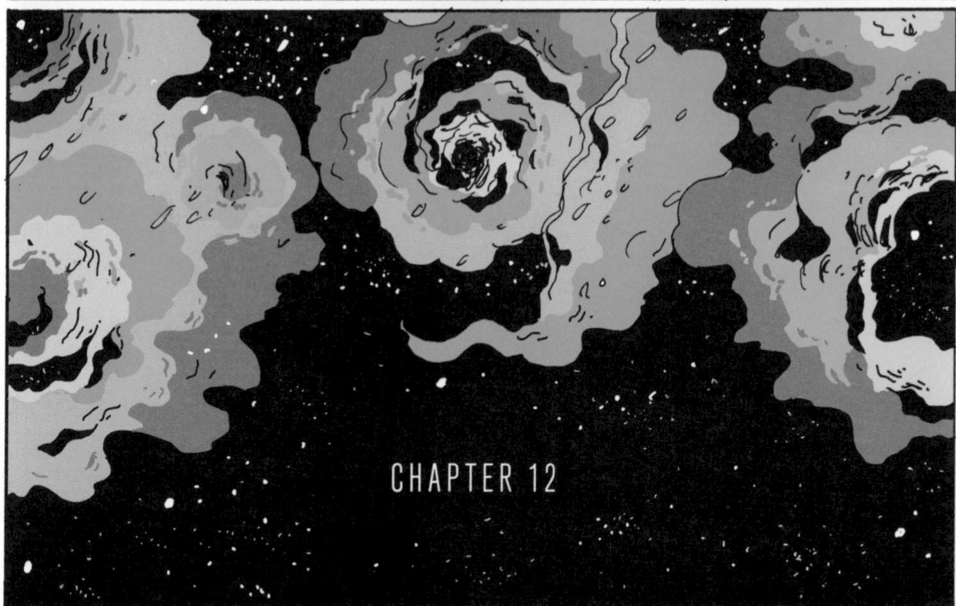
CHAPTER 12

I'm Mia.
You must
be...

Well, obviously, we got
the wrong room.
You're
joking.
SERIOUSLY,
Mattie?

This is ALL
Grace's stuff.
hmm
Her blanket.
Her posters.

Yeah, I guess you're
right. This looks like
her writing on the
floor.
AHH HER
STORY

She'll get
upset if she
sees the pages
out of order!
We KNOW that!
PICK IT UP!
This tore...
HURRY!

Put them back NEATLY!
Oh, hell.
Wow, she's written a lot.
It's really good.
SHE LET YOU READ IT?
Uh, yeah.
I need to ask you a few questions. It's Mia, right?
Right.
I'm Jane.

Just to confirm—
this is Grace's room?
yes
And where is Grace?

I'm not telling.
Why?
You're going to take her away.

Where'd you get that necklace, Mia?

Uhh, Janey?
The doorknob is moving.

Grace
You got taller.
Stay BACK! I'm not going!

I mean it, Jane!
I believe you.
Mia! Do something!
FUCK!
OW
Gracie

It's been a year since I last saw you.

Can I at least get a hug?

Helen's right. You did get taller.

What's happened? Why are you here?
I'll explain everything.

LITTLE SHIT
RRRRRRR
Little help over here?!

Let Mia GO! Helen, Mattie! Get OFF HER!
She HIT ME!
I don't CARE!

Grace

Are you okay?
Not really.

Are you okay?
Not at all.

ohhhh
okay, Grace
What?

You two are a THING!
Grace!! Your first girlfriend! Why didn't you tell us?
Grace!

What a great pair.
We are so proud of you.
Im glad Grace has someone strong looking out for her.
ohmyGOD stop you are so embarrassing.

Mom is going to be thrilled.
Mom?

Is... Is Mom OK?

We need to talk, Grace. Privately.
What's wrong?
Mia, you should step out.

She's staying. Now tell me.

The situation at home has Changed. The house... well, we had to leave it.
We've moved underground.

Mom got hurt during the move. We were attacked and she fell off her horse.
She can't walk anymore, but She's fine. Still running the whole show.

But...the fighting is bad and the borders are a mess. And we realized... well, **Mom** realized...

It's only getting worse. The land... everything is starting to deteriorate. It could make the edges of The staircase impossible to cross.
Basically...

...if you don't come home now... You might never be able to make it back.

Mom knows... we all know, that we promised you could finish school here.
But with everything going on...
She just wanted you home.
The house? was it destroyed?
Some parts are broken, but for the most part it's ok. Just empty.
And I know all your friends are here, and—
No one here likes me except for Mia.

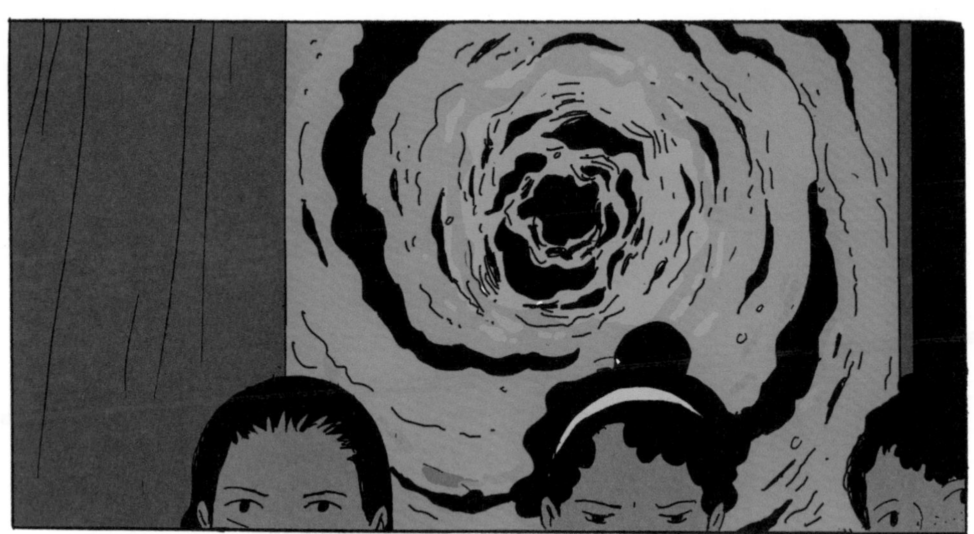

okay

okay?
OKAY?
What ELSE am supposed to Do?
You could fucking STAY.
I need time to pack.
You can have the night. But we need to leave by seven am sharp.

That was so fucking easy for you, wasn't it?!
You don't know ANYTHING!
That's enough!
You need to cool it, kid.
FUCK YOU!
Mia! Wait—
Grace—I would give Mia some space.
Just GO! I'll be ready in the morning.
Don't go after her. It's not a good idea.
She needs—

You don't KNOW her, you don't know what she needs.
Grace...
We're stronger than you think. I'm going to find her.
I'll see you in the morning.

Where are you?

Mia!
Grace?
Shh
Gr—
About fucking time.
I thought Grace was GONE! We're gonna get in trouble!
Shh
Just MOVE.

How did you even get the keys?
My sister snatched them, duh.
Ow! She fucking bit me!
Shh!
Get her IN.
Lock it!
I AM
Hurry!
SHUT UP, OH MY GOD!
There!
Shit
HEY
Sucks to suck.
haha
See you later!

Cristine, I fucking know you're there.
Let me OUT.
oops, sorry. Don't want to.
What the fuck is this place?
Cristine! You coming?
I'll catch up. You go ahead to dinner.
Cristine! I have to get to Grace! Please!

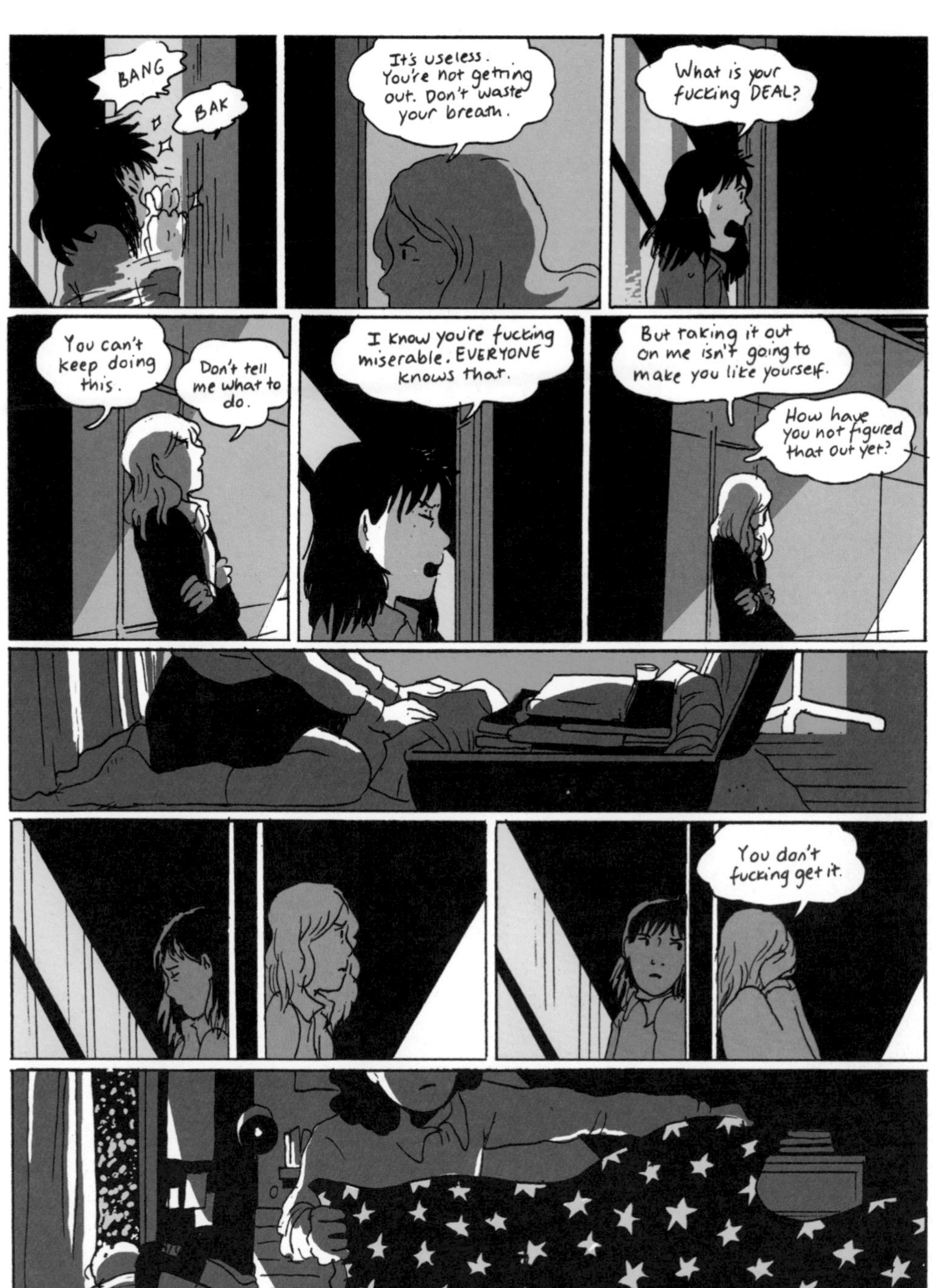
BANG
BAK
It's useless. You're not getting out. Don't waste your breath.
What is your fucking DEAL?
You can't keep doing this.
Don't tell me what to do.
I know you're fucking miserable. EVERYONE knows that.
But taking it out on me isn't going to make you like yourself.
How have you not figured that out yet?
You don't fucking get it.

Right. You're the only person in the world who's ever had a shit time.
That's not what I said.
Have you ever even tried the other way?
What?
Like, being NICE. Instead of trying to destroy every-one around you.
I'm not STUPID. I tried that. I was a sweet fucking kid and EVERYONE took advantage of that.
I won't let that happen again.
wow you ARE stupid.
You freak, you can't talk to me like that.
Shit doesn't always work. You can try again.
It may not have worked when you were a kid, but you're not a kid anymore.

You can start now, you know.
You could open the door...
Screw you.
Cristine!
Cristine!

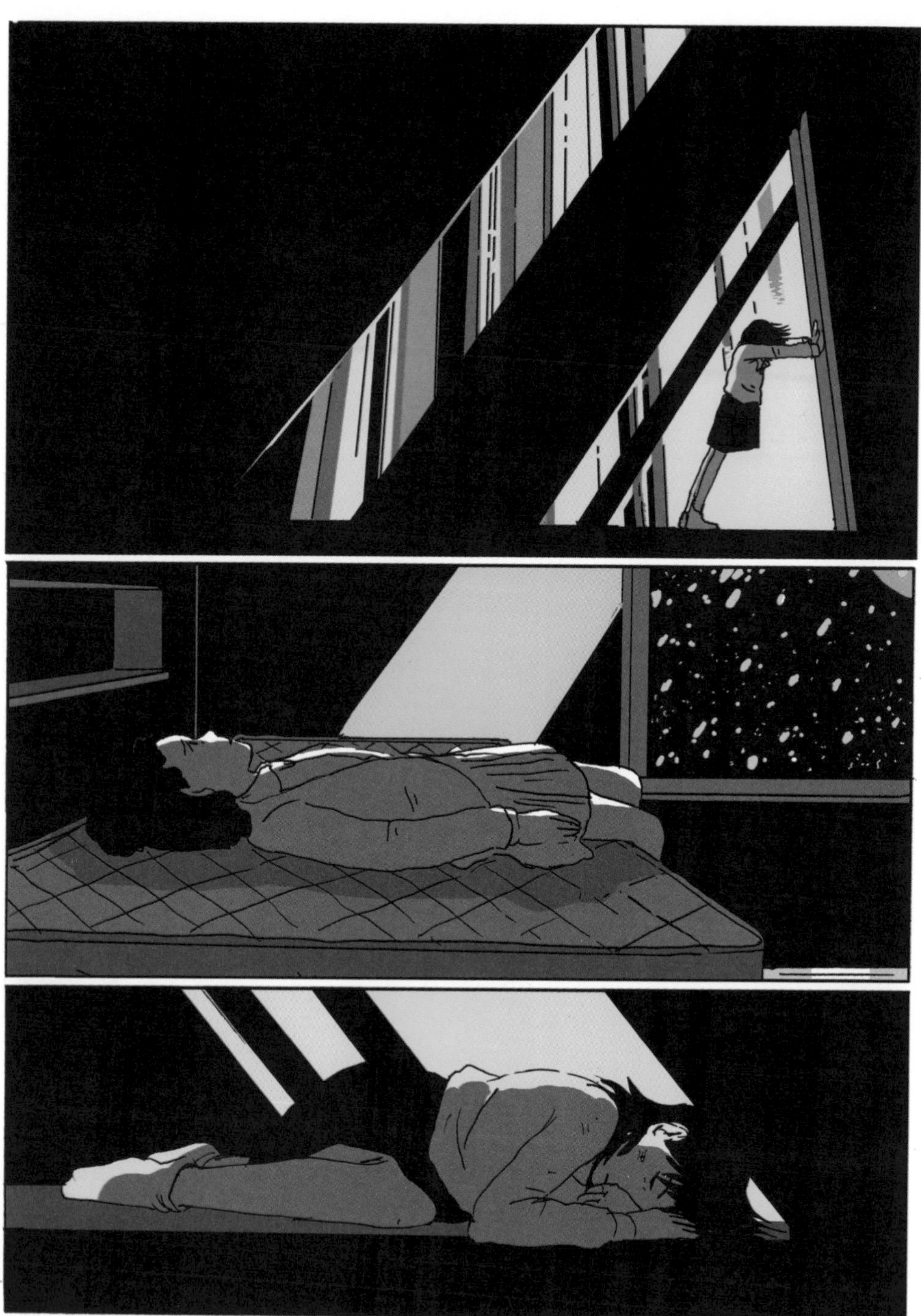

Gracie.
Time to go.
Not yet. Mia is coming to say good-bye.

Grace.
WAIT.

Don't let go!
I'm not! I've got you.
I've got yo
We'll make it out eventually.

Time's up, Grace.

Come on. Let's get you home.

I got her

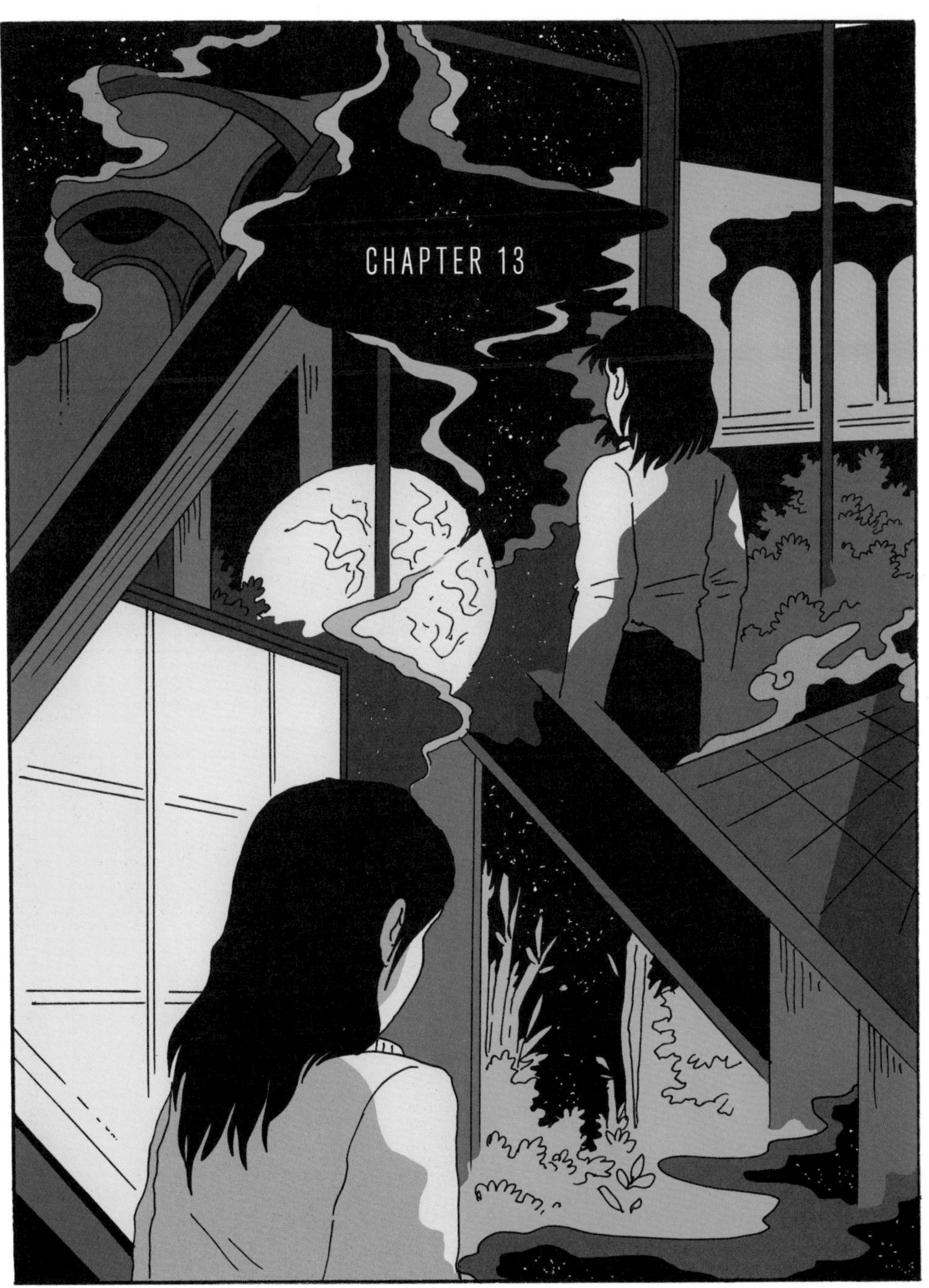
CHAPTER 13

I tried to get
in touch with her,
stupidly.

I still didn't really understand where she had gone. I tried sending her things, bugged the principal for info. But nothing would ever reach her. Where she lives... well, it's totally closed off.

And I know this is completely insane.
And you can say no.
But Ell...
Ell has their ways to get in touch with people in TS.
And... well now we know the location of one of Grace's Sisters. Helen.
That's all we could find out. But chances are where Helen is...
But, look, it doesn't really make any sense. It's been more than five years since I last saw her. She could be, you know, with someone. Happy, moved on.
I just... I just want to–
What? What do you want?

So, let me just see if I've got this right.

You want us to infiltrate one of the most deadly and secluded areas of space...

...to talk to this girl?

I get it.

Quiet, Jules.

Well, when you say it like that it sounds even crazier.
I'm sorry. This was so... selfish of me.

This is my own problem. I'll deal—
Mia.
I'll deal with it.
Mia.

Of course we'll go. We can't have you doing this all on your own.
Fuck yeah. I'm in.

What? You mean it?
Absolutely.

Jules, get the ship in the dock. We need to pack up—quietly.
Yessir!
You mean, we're going NOW?
But our jobs... YOUR job, Alma...

If Char were here she'd say we're all being impulsive...
But doing the "safe" thing... the "right" thing... that got us all screwed.
I'm done with that. We'll do this.

And we'll do it because we want to.

All right, bring it in. Mia, you look like you could use a hug.
I COULD USE A HUG.

OK. Let's get ready to go.

We have a stop to make before we start our next can job.
There it is.

Did you get Paul?
Already on the ship.

Fuel?
Jacked it all.
I think we're set.

WHAT IS GOING ON?

ew

Come on, let's leave. We don't have to explain ourselves.
Actually, I have a few words I'd like to say.

Where in God's name have you all BEEN?!
You know, I'd recommend starting a convo with "hi" or "howdy."
This place needs to be finished in TWO WEEKS.

Or, and I know this is probably a reach for you, a "how are you?"
That's IT. You are all done. I'm getting a new crew out here.

Hey, Alma, looks like we just got fired.
oops
This sure is a pickle.

I really don't fucking understand this.
What?
THIS

All of you have been rude, insubordinate, and just plain shits since I got here. I don't deserve this!
Jo, Jo.
I think you're forgetting a key part of this puzzle.

I'll admit that I have, at times, been slightly jerkish to you. But only for excellent reasons.

This is ridiculous.
No way, you stay RIGHT here and listen to me. Do you remember the night you showed up here?
Yes. So?

We were pissed when you showed up. Char was gone and we were broken. And we could've just taken that out on you.
But we didn't. You showed up and Alma made you dinner. We made you a bed, even played cards together.

And we TOLD you, we told you that Ell didn't talk, we told you their pronouns.
And you IGNORED US.

I don't need to know that stuff! This is a job, none of that is important.
No. No way. You don't get to decide that.

You don't get to decide what's important for US. You can choose for yourself, but no one else.
Fuck yeah, Jules.

When you chose not to respect us, we chose not to respect you.
The fact that you expect people you shit on to treat you nicely shows just how delusional you are.
I can't believe this. So I screwed up some words. You act like I'm a monster!
Wow... you, you really don't get it, do you?
Have you ever even considered that something that's trivial to you could mean... so much more to someone else?
You don't get to take the easy road out and just respect the parts of people that you recognize.
And, pro tip: If you find yourself in a similar situation in the future where you're surrounded by people you don't understand—
Try listening. It'll work a lot a better for you than talking.

I already contacted headquarters. A new crew is on its way.

I'm coming for you, Char. Just wait a little while longer.

Brought you coffee.
You're a Saint.
I'm assuming you won't be sleeping till we get there.
Correct.
That was great, you know. What you said.
Ahh, stop.
I mean it.
I'm so proud of you. I... I don't think I say that enough.

Don't say shit like that to me. It makes me miss Mom too much.

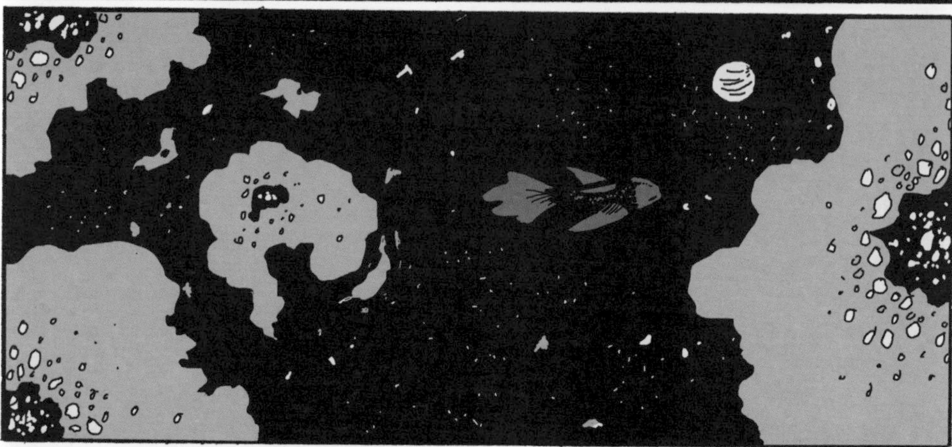

I ran out of hot chocolate making yours so I gave you extra whipped cream.
Gorgeous.

You good?
Golden. Glad to be gone.
That's poetic.

Can I ask you something?
Shoot.

Was the rest of school totally shit for you? After Grace left?
Why do you ask?
Dunno, it's just... Well, you seemed sad when you first got here. I didn't know if that was because of Grace.

When I got here? It feels like ages ago... I think I did feel mixed up. Maybe some of that was Grace. Maybe not.
But I mean... the rest of school...
haha
What?
It feels really strange to think about, but the rest of school was really...
Good. It was good. I was happy.

I mean, right after she left I was a mess. I completely fell apart.

But I came back. Misery seemed so useless. And the next school year I roomed with some good friends, joined more sports.
I played on our Lux team. My friend Abby joined, too. We lost every game and it was so much fun.

Oh, and that girl, the bully? Cristine? We got to be pretty tight, if you can believe it. We hung out a lot in senior year.

There were still holes, though, you know.
I didn't date anyone seriously. I kissed some random girls but none of it lasted.
And I avoided all the dances and parties. I just... Couldn't.
But really, overall, they were happy years.
But—oh GOD, at the end of school it was SUCH a mess. I had straight C's in EVERYTHING. No college would accept me and I was freaking out.
But at the last minute... well, my teacher... it was all because of her.

These rejection letters are just a polite way of saying "we don't fucking want you."
Mia, be civil.
It's useless, Ms. Martinez. I'll just have to go home and live with my moms.
There is... something. I don't know if it would suit you, or if you'd even like it...
What is it?

It's construction. Well, reconstruction. Restoring old buildings.
My baby sister runs a team of sorts. They travel a lot, so you'd get to see new places. And my sister... well, she's a character. The rebellious one in the family.
But Alma... well, she'd take good care of you.
I'd have to call her and see if she has room. But it could be a good thing for you, and it'd give you some time to figure things out.
I didn't know you had a sister.

I'm the oldest. Alma's the baby, and my middle sister, Rosa, she... She passed away. Alma and I haven't spoken much since.
Oh, I... I'm sorry.
But I'll call her for this. If you're interested.
Why would you do all that for me?
Do you remember the first time we met?
You were just ten. And it was your first day at Cleary's.

I found you walking through some back hall. Miles from where you should've been.
where are you headed?
My new room.
Do... you know where your room is?
Not yet. I'm still looking.
Wait—hold on!
Oh, GOD, I do remember that. My moms were flipping out cause I'd wandered off.
I got you back to them.

And I just remember thinking that if I hadn't found you, you would've just kept on walking.
I saw so much strength in you. So much courage.
I still do. And I want to help you see that in yourself.
What was your sister's name again?

Make sure you eat three meals a day, Mia.
Mom...
Are you sure this job is safe?
It's fine!
I just want to make sure you get properly fed! No skipping breakfast, okay?
I KNOW, Mom.
Will you call us?
YES, Mom.
You can come home anytime.
Anytime.
I know.

WAKE UP!
HELL
We're here!
You still haven't told me where "HERE" is.
Alma's house.

AHH! GRASS!
Char.

CHAPTER 14

Let's go, you three! Time to eat!
Breakfast!

Slow down, Jules...

Alma, should we...?
Right. Listen up, team.

We've had a few days to rest but it's time to get organized. The Second Winter hits The Staircase in two months and we do **not** want to deal with that.

If we can make it happen, I'd like to push off in two weeks.

Ell and I have just about finished the plan to get in and our routes when we're there.

What's the gist?

Start with the Surface. Do a sweep of the Hill lands and see if we can find anything.

But that's really just to be thorough. Most likely she's underground because of the weather. And our intel says Helen was seen down below, too.

That's gotta be a massive area to cover. What's the timeline?

One month, max. We'll cover as much as we can in that time...

But whether or not we find her, we're leaving when those three months are up. That's all we'll have supplies for, anyway.
we'll find her.
we'll try.

We meeting in here?

Yep, come on in.

Get settled, everyone.
I'm settled.

haha
AHHH

FOCUS! We have a lot to go through and NOT a lot of time.

That's better. Now. Who needs a refresher on TS? Or do we all know the basic history?

I don't know anything!

OK. We'll cover it all. Pay attention.
The Staircase is the region at the farthest edge of Space. It's roughly the size of Earth's moon, though the majority is uninhabited.
TS was discovered and colonized by the Hill family. They're officially recognized as the owners of all that land, and the family has been there for generations.
But when TS was still in its early days, there was a lot of conflict.
The Hills figured out pretty quickly that the land itself was something special. Full of healing rock, hot mineral water, and a ton of indigenous wildlife that can't survive anywhere else.
And of course... when other planets heard about the resources that their own moons and lands couldn't produce...
...they tried to take it. Take the rocks to heal their cities, take the water to wash toxins out of the air...

But the Hills would have none of that. TS's extreme weather was eroding their environment, but they'd persevered and stayed to protect the land. For its beauty, the animals, and, well...
It was their home. They wouldn't just let people come in and trample over it.
When the Hills turned down all the offers to join treaties or sell out, everyone shunned them.
This entire galaxy wrote a joint law making TS illegal. No one could go near it.
TS responded by doing the same. They closed their doors to every other world.

The relationship between TS and outside is tense, to say the least. Planets send assassins to take out the Hills, thinking without them they'll finally get access to TS and all its resources.
But that would never work. The people who live in TS, about 100,000, are just as dedicated as the Hills are when it comes to protecting this environment.

And besides, no one understands that land better than those who live there.
Plenty of people go there with orders to steal—and simply get lost.
The staircase is a maze of valleys and lakes, waterfalls and cliffs.
And all the rock there is hollow. Full of tunnels and caves that lead to underground cities and oceans.
Most outsiders can barely navigate the surface, let alone all that's beneath it.

But luckily for us, we're going in there with a local.
And there's a lot of internal politics I'm not covering. But you'll know the basics.
All our electronics are useless there. They have their own system that fries anything we try to use.
We'll be splitting up at times to cover more ground. Ell will lead one team, I'll lead the other.
But when we go underground, we stick together. Ell makes the calls, no fighting about it.

All right. Beautifully told, babe. My turn. The ship needs to be cleaned out and we have to lose any excess weight. Clear out all books, games, and statues.
Char—can you search the attic for our winter gear? We're going to need it. Hats, jackets, boots, the works.
yep.
And you two—you need some training. We're going into **hostile** territory. Char and Ell could just about win any fight, but you two need to get ready.

WHY are we using sticks?

Just to get warmed up, then we'll move to hand to hand. We won't have any weapons, so that's where you'll need the practice.

Come at me, Mia.

Don't just charge straight ahead!
Watch me! Find my weak points!
There you go.
Come on in, Jules.
RAAAAH

Oh, no way, they're not ready for you.
What?! We can so take Ell down.
Fuck yeah!
oh god
Fine, both of you go at once. That way you almost have a chance.

Don't get discouraged. You're making progress so let's keep it up.

What ARE you?!

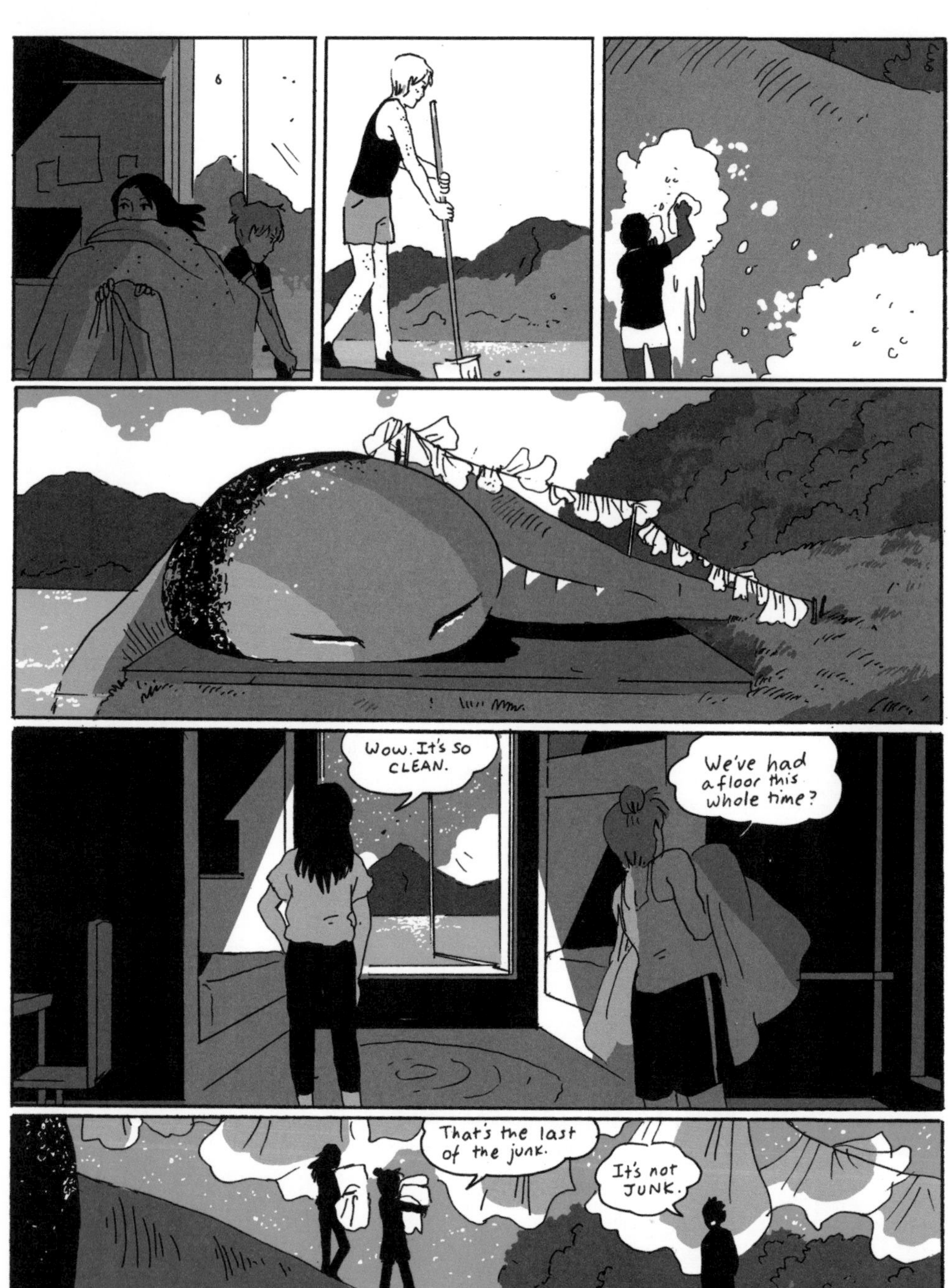
Wow. It's so CLEAN.
We've had a floor this whole time?
That's the last of the junk.
It's not JUNK.

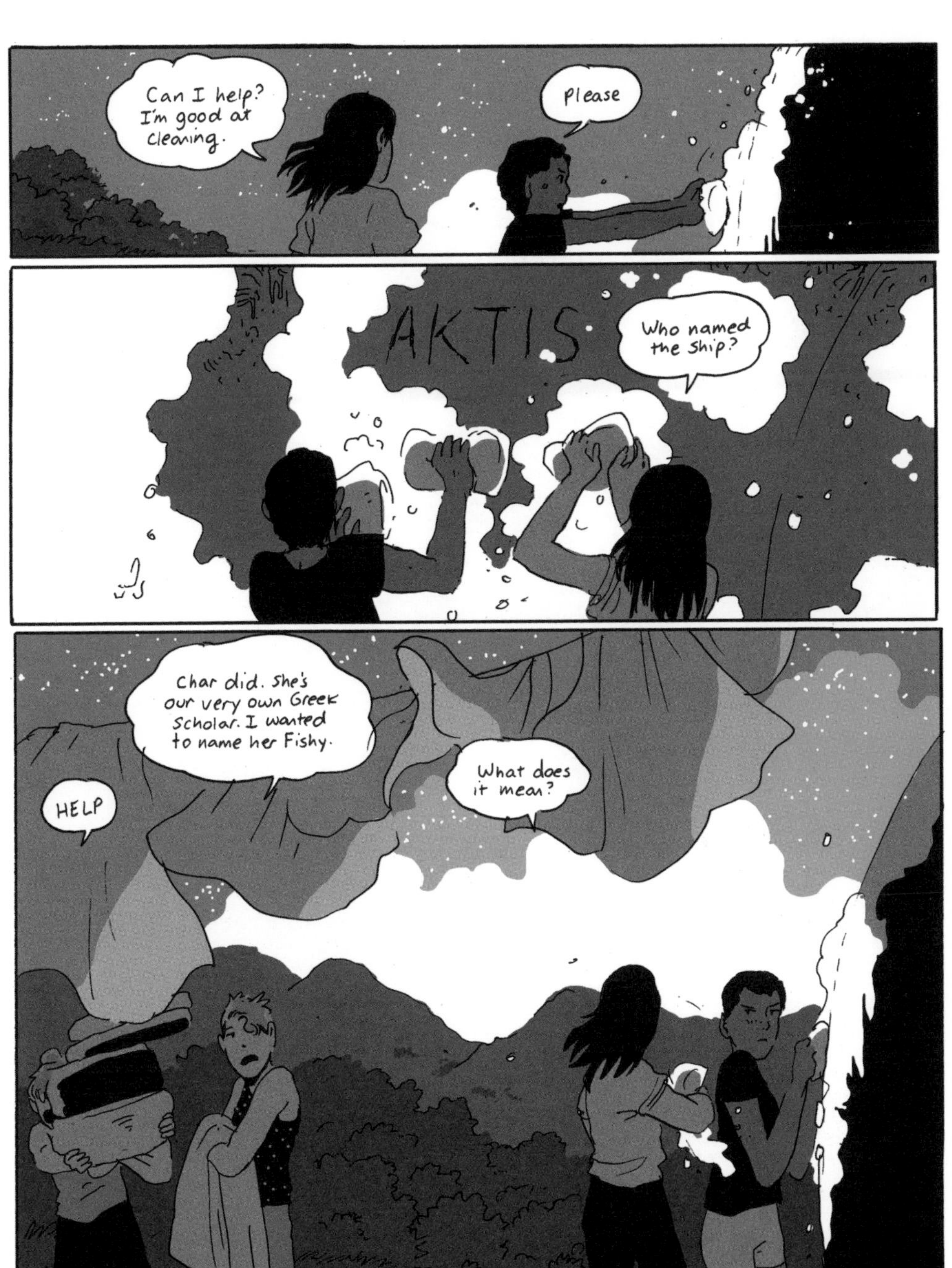
Can I help? I'm good at cleaning.
Please
AKTIS
Who named the ship?
Char did. She's our very own Greek scholar. I wanted to name her Fishy.
What does it mean?
HELP

sunbeam.

Hey
Hey you
You guys are up late.
I couldn't sleep. Alma's just staying up for me.
Are you guys sure about this? That you really want to...
Let me ask you this. If Jules needed your help, needed our help, would you support her? Even if it was dangerous?
Of COURSE I'd help her. But it's different, you've all known Jules a lot longer...
You're just as much a part of this family as Jules is. As any of us are.
I really love you guys.
I don't think we'd be doing this if we didn't love you just as much.

You didn't tell her yet, did you?
hmm?
Oh, now's my chance.
I didn't want to say anything in front of Jules... My sister made me promise not to talk to her about my years doing... not very legal things...
What?
We've met your Grace before. Me, Char, and Ell got hired to take the youngest Hill out of The Staircase and to a school.

we were only with her a few weeks. Almost got killed trying to get her out...
But we got her to school.

To you.

We got to her
Once, Mia. We can
get to her again.

Please fix
your jacket.
It's driving me
crazy.

Can one of
you do me a
favor?

Name it.

Do you know
how to cut
hair?

Get up! We're leaving!
Guhhh
Five more minutes
No way. We're leaving now.

You got a midnight haircut WITHOUT ME?!

You were sleeping!
NO EXCUSE!
EAT

You look fucking great but I'm still mad!

Come on, you three, we're pushing off in five.

Closed up?

All·right, kids,
let's do this.

CHAPTER 15

You need more layers. We're landing soon.
You're kidding. I'm already wearing a ton.

The air is going to be freezing and the dust that blows around is **sharp**.
FINE.

Jesus, it's huge...

SHHH
SHHH
WOW
SHH

WOW

The ship is in camouflage mode so we're good to go.
Jules, you're with me. Ell, you lead Alma and Mia.
Take these maps and mark the areas you cover. Add anything else you think we should know. Patrols, animals, loose rock, things like that.
We need to find out if people are still living on the surface. Ell said there used to be small towns between these cliffs. If they're still around, we'll find them.
Back at the cave in four hours. This is just the first sweep. Don't take any unnecessary risks.
Be safe.

There's the old Hill compound. Let's see if it's really abandoned.

Lead the way, Ell.

I'll check in here.
we'll sweep the hall.

creak
What—
creak

Do you think someone saw us come in here?
Could be...

Let's get out of here.
We still have to cover all the surrounding fields.

Something's wrong.
We don't know that.
They're more than an hour late!
I'm going to find th—
dammit

ah FRICK
Jules!
That bush was spiky!
I told you not to walk through it.

Where WERE you two?! I was losing my mind!
Ah jeez
Sorry, we got sort of stuck...
Sort of?
There was a patrol that almost saw us. We had to hide for a while until they cleared out.
We hid in this cave full of mud and our shoes got stuck. It took ages to get out...

Find anything useful?
Nothing. You guys?
Nada.
We think someone may have been following us, though.
I wouldn't be surprised.
Well, it's just the beginning. There's a lot still to cover, so let's get some sleep.

We've been looking out here for days. She's not here, Char. No one is.
She's right. No Way Grace is on the surface.
Everyone has moved underground. The towns that used to be here are gone.

Ell? What do you think?

Dammit. OK.

Pack as much as you can carry and we'll head to the opening that Ell found for us.

Once we head underground there's no coming back out until we either have Grace or decide to leave for good.
Getting in and out will be hell. We've only got one shot.

Dammit, I... I don't know about this. Jules, this is too dangerous for you to...
AS IF!

Alma—
You have no idea WHAT we're getting into, Jules. Listen to me—
BUZZ OFF, you're not my fucking MOM!

Keep your voices DOWN.
No, but I'm your GUARDIAN—
I don't CARE.

We've been in danger this WHOLE TIME, why is this any DIFFERENT?
Guys—
She's right, Alma.

Then you don't leave my side. Not even for a SECOND.
OK
Do you understand?
Yes, GOD.

We're all gonna stay together. No matter what.

OK.
OK.

Ahh... sorry
I, um, snapped...
Don't take your stress out on ME.
I'm sorry.
ooooh

All right, all right. Let's get a move on. I want to get to the opening before dark.

That's it.

Ell first. Then Mia, Jules, Alma, and I'll be at the back. Stay quiet, everyone.
Ell, whenever you're ready.

Ell! Behind us!

Ell! No—
Hey—

They're coming at us from both sides!

Who's over there?!
Shit! Here they come!

Mia–
come on!
Ell! Mia! Finish them and catch up with us!

I'll follow the others!

fuck

Alma! In here!
It's too small!
COME ON!
RUN, JULES!

That's all of them.

But the others went that way.

What are we—

Shit-

CHAPTER 16

Oh, no, no..
no thank you
no, wait—
Please... I...
I...

What do we do?
QUIET
There's too many of them.
I said QUIET.
Hey, come on, let's build a little trust here. You want to know why we're here, right?
We'll find that out soon enough.
Well, I'll make your job a little easier. I'll tell you, I just need something in return.
Oh, really?
That kid with us, just... when you find her, bring her to us.
That won't be possible.
Why?!
Alma-
What does that mean?

No one's going after her. She chose a bad crack to go down.
Why?! What's down there?
That's enough!
No, FUCK, you staircase people are supposed to be fierce. Show some balls and go GET HER—
COWARDS
SLAM
Jesus...
You ok?
I guess.

Elliot!
Where are we going?!
Ell, I'm worried about them. We have to go back.
You can't just ignore me, Elliot—

We need a PLAN.
Go find Grace
Well no shit, what about—
Elliot—
WHERE are you going?

How long are they gonna leave us in here?
As long as they want to.
Please don't say "I told you so."
Come on, I wouldn't do that...
Alma.
hmm
what are we doing?
we're helping her.
No, no, not that...
And cut the holy act. I know you want to help Mia but that's not the only reason we're here.
Excuse me?
You live for this shit. I know you miss it—the danger, the adrenaline of the jobs we used to do.

I—
Ok, fine, but that's only a SMALL part of it.
I'm not judging. We all have our own reasons for doing this...
But I meant... well.. what are we doing?
You mean us?
We've been working so much, for so long.
Are you unhappy?
No. That's what's strange. I am happy.
But that doesn't mean things should stay the same.
I feel like we haven't had any time.
Time to just be together.
Time to rest.

Am I making any sense?
You always make too much sense.

Maybe... we could...

...maybe we could. We could.

Hey.

HEY. Little buddy, pal. You better be showing me to the exit.
I swear to God, this better not be some bullshit afterlife place...

Well?
How about you do me a solid and take me to my friends?
I don't have time for your little "journey." I have a couple to reunite, goddammit.
Shit. I am so screwed.

FuckFUCKfuck.
I'm so dead.
I should've done more drugs... kissed more girls... eaten spicier food...
My obituary is gonna blow... Here lies Jules, that girl who punched some ice skaters and worked on buildings that no one cares about...
Ell and Mia are probably okay...
cough
Hey, Marshmallow. We making any progress toward that exit?

Oh nonono
Get OFF!
Fucking Staircase goddamn!

Hello?

Hello? Is someone out here?
Hello?

where are you?
RAAHHH
I can't do this.
I can't... I can't breathe
where are you...?

I can't believe this!
Seriously, I told her already.
I believe you!
Mattie's just forgetful.
That's an understatement.

Jesus, NO, I am not going to be defeated by these goddamn flying blueberries!
No way.
whoa

HAH! Fucking right. I win, you creeps.

Jane!
No one fucks with me.
No one—
uh

knock
Unbelievable.
You made it.
You really made it.

Get in here—quickly.
No one saw you, I suppose?
Here, here, sit. Get warm.
There's some stems by the fire. You still smoke?
Good God...
I still can't believe you're here...
It's just been so long...
Eight years...
Sid would've loved to see you all grown up.

But Elliot...
As happy as I am to see you...
You know better than this. You shouldn't have come back.
It may have been a few years but as soon as someone recognizes you... you won't leave here alive.

We'll see about that.

CHAPTER 17
Let's go, Elliot.
Is the ink packed?
I think so.
Check.
It's all here.

Where's your hat?
Don't need it.
You'll get dust in your hair.
I know.
Your parents probably wouldn't approve of me letting you get so ragged...

Everyone still agrees that Sid was the best map maker TS has ever seen.
And all that mystery around her, my God. All those rumors.
Everyone wanted to know how she did what she did. But no one ever saw her work.
Except for you.
Get the emerald ink ready.
Mix it slower this time.

Bring it over...

And watch how I do this.

You'll need to finish these maps someday.

But I bet we could—
No.

There isn't enough time for me.

But there's time for you.

She taught me everything.
My sister was Brilliant, there's no denying that.
So, why?
Why...?
Sid?
Why did we go down there?
What the hell was she thinking?
Quickly, Elliot.
We have work to do.

She knew what she was doing and she knew what might happen.
It was her life's work. She needed to finish it...
The monument... did it ever get built?
Elliot, you can't be thinking..
The monument is in the Square, in the **middle** of town.
You'll be recognized immediately! And as soon as they realize you're back, every person in The Staircase will be after you!
I'm tired of being blamed.
Come on, Elliot...
I love you like my own, but you know that what happened won't ever be forgiven here.

Stay close to me, Elliot.
And have the paper ready.
If I could do it all again...
I wouldn't change a thing.
I'd do it again. I'd do it a thousand times.

sid?
sid?

You killed an Ancient Being, Elliot!
There is no greater crime here.

You took something from a world beyond our own!
And it took Sid! It took Sid from my world!

I... should go.
Please, Elliot. Don't go to the monument.
I worked so hard to get you out. To make sure the fate TS wanted for you would never happen.
I got you a new life.
Don't throw that away.

Elliot
Thank you for everything.

I...am sorry. You shouldn't be here.
You...talk.
This is the first time I have ever needed to.

uh...
Why is that?
No one has ever come this far.
This should not have happened.
Well, biscuits, it DID.
And now you have to HELP me.
There would be no point.
The last time humans came close to me lives were lost. Changes were made.

The air here.
It is not meant for you.
Breathe a small amount and you will be ill.
But you have made it all the way to me. You have come too far, and you will not last long.

Just...
I'm so tired.
Just
Don't tell me any more, okay?
I don't want to know.
All... all I want...
Is for you to get me out of here...
...and back to my friends.

Well?!
You are not like the ones from before.
What can I say, I'm a unique gal. Now show me the way out of this creepy forest spirit basement.
Marshmallow.?
She will guide you out.

You're the little Shit that led me into this *literally* deadly place.
You've got one chance to make it up to me.
All right
Hey, hold on a sec.

So you don't... have some cool trick or... meds that could maybe get this air out of me?
Yeah, ok. ok. That's what I thought.
Ok, bud, I need you to find my friends—
And I need you to go quick.

Here she is, ma'am. One of the group of five.
Take a seat.
Ms. Hill...
I... I don't know if you remember me... My name is Char.
We met when Grace ...
No need to say any more.
All of you, leave us.
Wait! I—

Could they...bring Alma here? The woman with me?
If she's here I'll tell you anything you want to know.
Bring her.
Yes, ma'am.
Now.
Because of what you did for my Grace all those years ago, I'll listen to you.
So please, tell me why you're trespassing in my home.

SID GE

Unbelievable.
Everyone said you were dead.
You aren't getting away this time.
Word is out, Elliot. Everyone knows you're here.
You're dead.
* cough*

Faster.
You've gotta go faster.
char!
Ma'am, a word...
You ok?
I am now that you're here.

Where?
The monument. Elk Square.
I'm afraid I can no longer speak with you ladies.
What—
Ms. Hill—
SILENCE.
You failed to mention to me that one of your associates...
was Elliot Reed.

Hurry...
hurry
What's the problem?!
Lock them back up.
Wait!

Find them. Bring Elliot to me, am I clear?
Yes, ma'am!
It's time that they paid for what they did.

You need to cool it, kid.
FUCK YOU!

Mia... what are you doing here?

Grace. I need to see her. Talk to her.
You need to take me to her.
Why would I do that? It's been what, four years?
Five years.
And you came all this way?
You're... insane.
Please, Jane.
What's your plan?? Steal her away? Run off together?
You must be delusional to think—
No.

I just want to talk to her.
That's all.
Hurry!
Dammit!

Dammit, we're not here to do any harm, just—
Wait— what is that?

Jules!

Okay. I'll take you to her.
Follow me.

CHAPTER 18
ENOUGH!

All of you, quiet down!
And back up!
You—what was your name?
Alma
And this girl?
Jules
Ok. I need you to listen to me, Alma.
And I need you to stay calm. Can you do that?
Yes

What's wrong with her?

She was with a Tessian Fox, our oldest creature.

She must have gotten past our barrier. The air past that point is toxic. By the look of her, she's breathed far too much of it. She's quite sick.

Tell me how to make her better.

She's comatose at this point. All you can do is wait and see if she wakes up.
Does your ship have medicine on it?
Yes.
I'll give you a horse so you can get her to it.

...and you.
Y-yes

Lock her back up.
Yes, ma'am.

I—
Wait—

I'll help this child, but the rest of your little **group** is still at large.
Once we've captured Elliot we can speak again.

Can I just...

...say good-bye to my wife...

Fine, hurry up.

I'll find the others.
I'll get the ship and bring it to the entrance we came in.
We'll meet you there.
Why are you all standing around?! Where's that horse?

I don't know who your girl is—

But taming and... connecting with a Tessian Fox is something no one here has ever been able to do.

She must be extraordinary.

She is.

You hang in there!

Think.
Think.
Killer!
Where'd they go?!
Over here!
How far are we?
Still a ways to go.

Killer!

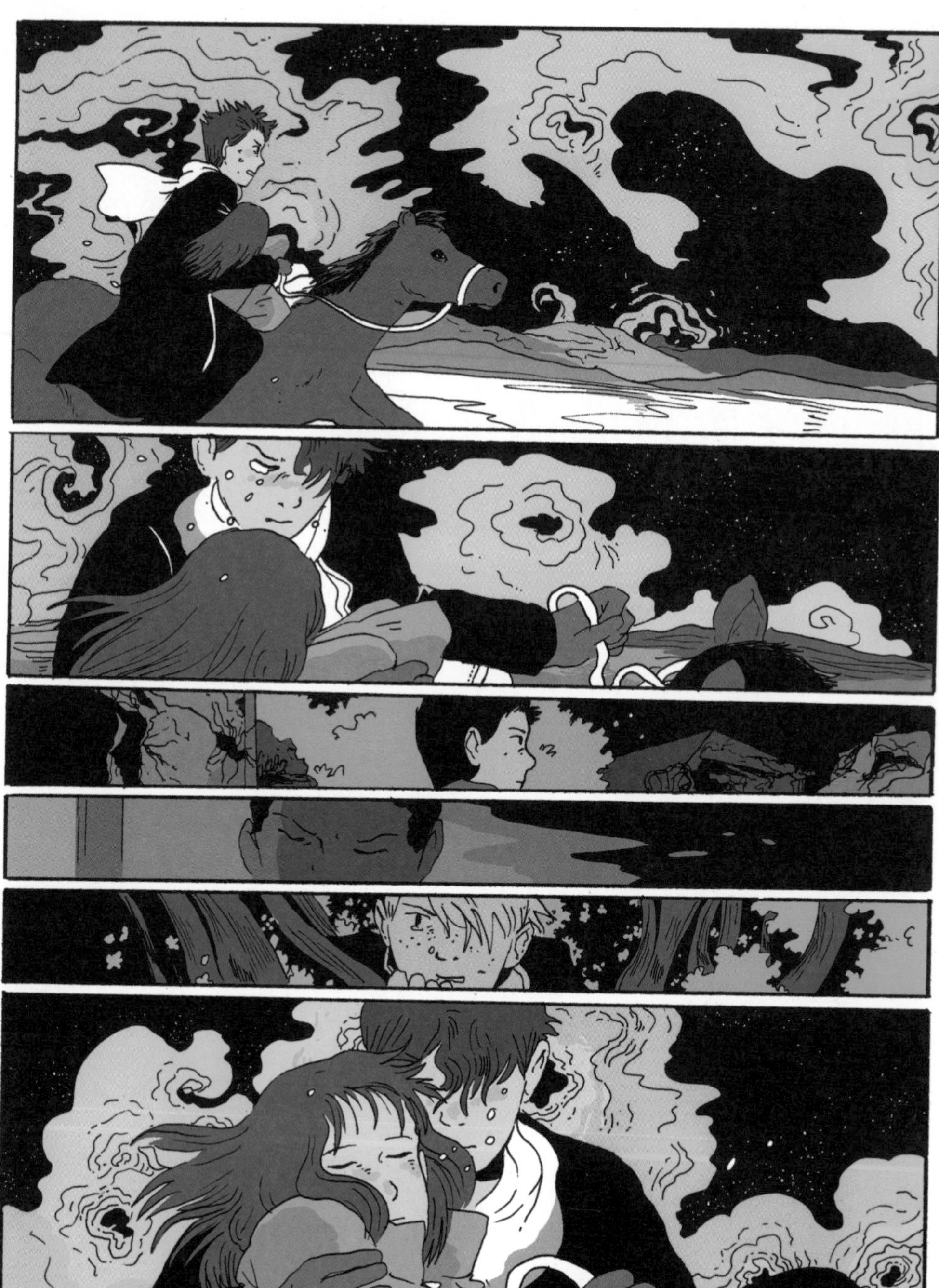

You're headed there now?
Yeah, I'm gonna give Ellen a break.
She's been watching her cell all day. Besides, I haven't gotten to see any of the intruders yet...
You're ridiculous. See you at dinner?

Running out of time...
FUCK!

Almost there...

We're almost there...

Think, think, think...
HEY—
CRASH
THUP
creak

Elliot!

Ell, oh, God!

You're here.

What—Jesus, Ell, there's so much blood.

Elliot, listen. Jules is sick. Alma has her and is gonna fly the ship to the cave entrance we came in. We have to meet them there.

Down here!
Come on!

Ell, wait!

Mia isn't with you?

There they are!

They're catching up!

Ell! We can't stop! Ell–
I got you–
Just a little farther...

This is it.

Go up the stairs and make a left down the hall.
You'll know her room when you see it.

Knock

Go away, Jane. I'm BUSY.

CHAPTER 19

What is so important, Jane, I'm—
Jane is... downstairs. I'm sorry, I didn't mean to interrupt or... startle you.

Mia? What—
How are you... are you insane?
I...
Your hair is shorter than it used to be.
I cut it pretty recently.

I don't—
I mean,
why...
How did you make it this far? I mean... God, WHAT are you doing here?
I...
I'm here for... you.

Because I ***did*** know you.

I knew you and I—

I didn't get to say good-bye.

And when you left, after what your sisters said...
I didn't know... and I couldn't find out...
What?
If you were STUCK. If you came home and had no way back **OUT**.
And I'm not here to just pick up where we left off. You have to believe that.
We're not in love and we're not kids. Not anymore.
This is something completely new.

My friends and I came a really long way and—
Friends?
Yeah. Four of them.
You've always been good at that.
At what?
Making friends.
They could be your friends, too.

We go everywhere. We live on the ship together and fly to buildings that we fix up ourselves.
If there's any-where you want to go, we cangive you a lift. Or if you just want to write and tag along... you're welcome.
And I don't want to assume anything. Every-thing could be great for you here and you don't need to change that, I just...
I couldn't come all the way here and not at least tell you that... that there's room for you.

But there's no pressure, I... I would be happy to just...
...to say good-bye.
I can't believe you came all this way just to say that...you could've been killed... and I...
I... I can't just leave.

I'm working on my play and the stars haven't lined up and everything is...
I don't, I mean, I can't—
Grace.
I'm only on the first draft, I—
Grace.
It's ok. I understand
Why didn't you come that day? My last day? You could've said good-bye then and you wouldn't have had to—
I tried!
That day. I tried to get to you in time, you have to believe me.
And I did make it to you.

It just took five years.
You always did have the tendency to be tardy...
That hasn't really changed.
I... I don't want to keep you from your writing.
Oh, I...
I can't begin to explain how happy it makes me to see that you're okay.
Take this.

Bye, Mia.
Kat is going to show you out of the caves. Quietly, okay, Kat?
Got it.

Thank you, Jane.
Get back safely.

We're almost there!
Hang in there, Ell!

They better be there...
Gracie?

She's up there!
Alma! Land the fucking ship!
What—Elliot! Shit—
Hurry! Get on the ship, they're right behind us!
Char!
Where is Mia?!

Jules?
She's breathing but no sign of waking up.
Elliot, christ!
Alma, they're still coming after us. We need to move the ship!
Where the fuck is Mia?
I don't know.
Alma! What do we do?
Get us up high! Stall!

Fuck, NO!
Char, get the ship up higher!

They're not going to stop! They know Ell is on this ship!
And I can't fix this many stab wounds; Elliot is going to bleed out!
what do we do?

we need
to leave.

we're not
far...

What...
No, that... that can't be...

That's... that's OUR SHIP!
Where are they going?!
Guys! Wait! FUCK!
ALMA!
CHAR!
JULES!
ELLIOT!

NO!
FUCK!
WAIT!

...they wouldn't leave me...

You need a flare.
That'll get their attention.

I'll send it up.
Jane, this bag is heavy. Can you get it?

what-

Mia, are you crying?
I—

Alma!

It's blue! That means it's friendly!
what if it's a trap?!

Turn the ship around.

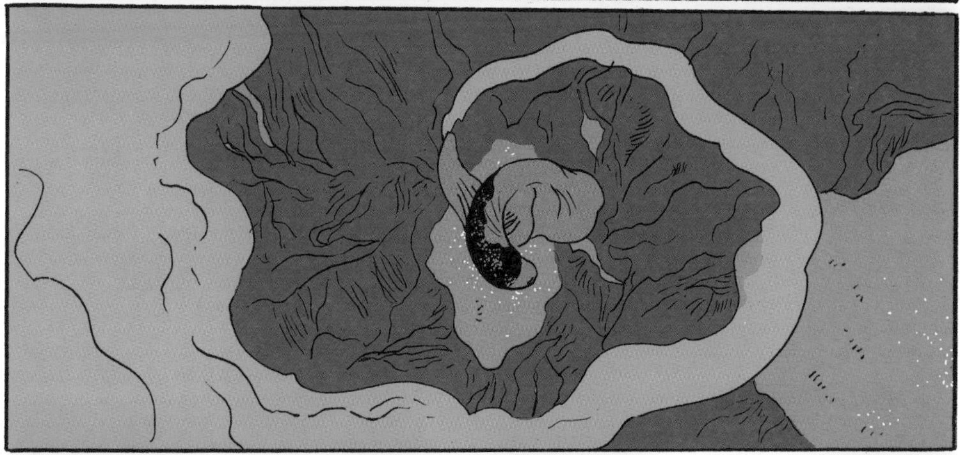

But you... you said...
I couldn't just make a decision right away. I had to think and talk to Jane.

You want to come with us?
I... want to try. You came all this way and... Well... let's not leave each other anymore, ok?
Deal.

I sent word to let this ship past the border.
You'll do great.
Follow me.

Ohmy GOD
what HAPPENED?

What up, queen?

You're late.
Jesus Christ
did you two
fight a WAR?!
Oh, thank God.
She's fine,
she's fine!

Are you guys really ok?
I found this lollipop so I'm doing way better.

GODDAMMIT, MIA, I WAS SO SCARED!

I was, too.

Hello, there.

Um, everyone. There's someone you should meet.

Don't worry, I'll do all the talking.
Just take it one step at a time.
Everyone-
This is Grace.

CHAPTER 20

You don't think we'll be at a disadvantage?
Well, we'll have less power but we'll be faster.
That's true. But we don't actually have to do the side quest. We could just head straight for the tower.
We need the items, though. Isn't your sword broken from the last fight?
Yeah... and you need more arrows.
We should definitely do the side quest. We'll make a little money, too.
Yeah, we're poor as shit!
We could really use some help down here, you know.
And, Jules, did you reattach the wing?

I don't know what the poverty line is in this game. I'll look it up.
Mia, PLEASE, we are strategizing here.
I should never have let Jules get Grace into video games...
I think that's everything.
You think the remodel turned out ok?

Rewiring everything was so annoying...

But at least we have our own rooms. No more of Jules' snoring.
I heard that.

Is it time?

It's time.

Alma's totally gonna cry.

Did you check your list? You have everything?

We're all set.

Are you guys gonna be ok? Won't you get, like, bored?

We'll manage.
I want to swim in the lake and cook you dinner.
I'm gonna build you a new office.
I want built-in shelves.
Yeah. We'll be ok.
And you guys will be, too. Your new captain is going to take care of you.
I'll do my best.

Mia, Sheila will be expecting you in about a week. It should be an easy job with good pay.
We got you your first job, but after this one...
You're on your own.
We'll find something to do.

Ok, get out of here before I change my mind about giving you my precious ship.

Call us when you get there.

Take care of them.

I'll miss you, you loser.
Shut up. I'll miss you more.

Call anytime.
Anything you need. Just tell us.

I know there's work to do but Grace and I really want to start the next level...
mhmm
It's really life or death.
How long is this game?!

They don't know about Sid...or any of that, do they?
Don't worry. I won't say anything.
I studied the maps you two worked on. They're beautiful.
Fine, but only for an hour. Then we need to—
YESSSS
Come on, Grace!
Okay.
Shit!
UH—

Alma.
JULES!
They're spinning out of control!
Are you sure you finished bolting in the wing?! Both sides?
I FORGOT ABOUT THAT!

AHH! They're gonna CRASH!
It's gotta be the wing.
Yikes.
OK. OK.
Ell, get your tools. Jules, get the window at the top of the wing open.
Grace, over here.

On it!
You sit here.
Mia.
Hold on to this.
MIA!
Pull up gently. If we start falling fast, push this button.
I can't do this.
Sure you can.

Do you remember...
I'll never forget.
You don't have a great track record with flying machinery.

...crashing that ship at school? In the middle of the night?

I think you'll find I'm a little better than when I was fourteen.

Call me if a red light turns on. I need to go help Jules and Ell!

SHE'S NOT PICKING UP.
Just wait.
Pass me the wrench.
REALLY? Alma is CALLING ME.
Pull, Jules!
I am!

Almost there—
UH, MIA, HELP NOW PLEASE!

It's in!
Got it!

All right!
Yes!

They're ok.

We're not dead.
Not yet.
This was a great start. We're a raging success already.
That's one way to look at it.

Come on, Grace.
Let's start the next level.
Okay.
You can go with them, Ell. I'm just gonna get us on course, then I'll join y'all.

A huge thank you to Ricky Miller for working with me while **On a Sunbeam** originally came out as a slightly sporadic webcomic. And a big thanks to all you folks who read and supported this story in its early form.

As always, thank you to Connie Hsu for sticking by my side and helping me turn wild drawings into a real goddamn book. Thank you to everyone at First Second for all your support and hard work.

Thank you, Seth. Always and forever.

And thanks to my parents for continuing to cheer me on through all this.

♡

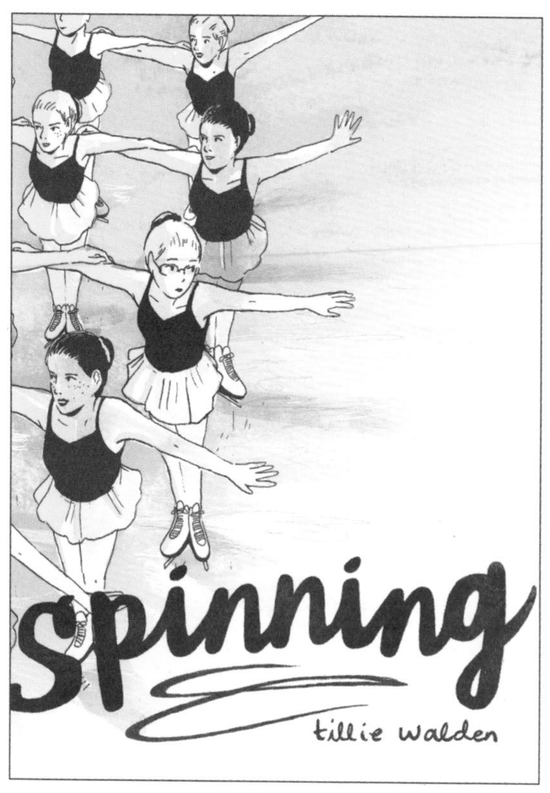

A.V. Club Best Book of the Year
Paste Best Book of the Year
Wired Best Comic of the Year

"This beautiful story about sorrow, growth, and triumph will resonate in every reader's heart."

—Laurie Halse Anderson,
New York Times–bestselling author and two-time National Book Award finalist

Tillie Walden is a cartoonist and illustrator from Austin, TX. She is the creator of the graphic memoir Spinning from First Second Books. She is also the creator of the Ignatz Award winning book The End of Summer and the Eisner nominated story I Love This Part. Tillie is a graduate of The Center for Cartoon Studies, a comics MFA program in Vermont.

For more information on Tillie and her work, please go to tilliewalden.com.

I LOVE GRAPHIC NOVELS!

Keep reading with these amazing books.

I want a book that's excitement and magic from start to finish!

I want a book that's thoughtful and realistic!

Please give me the most possible adventures.

Apocalyptic adventures!

Otherworldly adventures!

Historical adventures!

Magical stories FTW!

Magic and myth and self-acceptance!

Magic and family and identity!

Absolutely true stories!

About amazing women throughout history!

About ice skating, first love, and coming out!

Books belong in the kitchen.

Pie and hockey and more pie!

Bakery disasters and boyfriends!

The best books are kissing books!

Especially when you can kiss in gorgeous dresses!

Especially when there's dramatic family history!